HIGH-FIVE

— TO THE —

Hero

Frances Lincoln
Children's Books

Dear Reader,

At this year's Noble Monarch Jubilee, where leaders from fairy tales gathered to meet, it was my pleasure to debut my book *Power to the Princess*. It was a joy to see a wide audience of fairytale royalty and magical creatures find themselves in the pages of the book, and be inspired by one another's stories.

After the jubilee I received notes and messages from readers. I heard from teachers and librarians, kids, and grandparents, and to my great surprise from kings and queens! There were warm words, as well as questions, curiosities, and ideas. One remarkable letter was from four amazing men: King Midas, Pied Piper, Geppetto, and Anasi. Their letter was friendly and congratulatory yet also posed an important question.

Dear Ms. Murrow,

We spotted your book right away at the jubilee and after enjoying it ourselves, we selected it for our Dads' and Kids' book club. The children were delighted to revisit these familiar stories and see the women in them celebrated as admirable leaders.

The children now want to read more books like this! So, we went on the hunt for stories of our favorite heroes, princes, and kings.

But sadly, our collections fell short in this area. And the representation of these well-known characters is quite narrow.

Please will you write a book that celebrates the beauty and bravery of boys and men in our fairy tales?

I saw their point. Something *was* missing from their stories, so I accepted the challenge! Over the next few months, I met with heroes, princes, and kings to listen and learn. Each one told me of their experiences—how they broke the mold, changed the game, or discovered their purpose. Their stories included magic and sword play, hard work, and creativity. Some took a long journey or faced a great challenge. Others told of romance, friendships, or a special passion.

Each told me of a time they felt vulnerable and how they set their feelings free. About the importance of laughter and surprises and not always being right. All of their stories featured special helpers and mentors who supported them when they stood up for themselves or others, who helped them listen to their instincts.

I learned so much from these brave and beautiful men. What struck me the most was that the story of what makes a hero, a prince, or a king, is the story of what anyone can be. A hero is courageous of heart and gentle with themselves and others. A king feels deeply, listens actively, and laughs wholly with their community. A prince is a game changer who casts off expectations to fulfil their own purpose. Now that their stories have been retold, I invite you to turn the page and discover these real heroes, princes, and kings.

Vita Murrow

Adventures in This Book

LIST OF HEROES AND THEIR STORIES

King Arthur

Once upon a time, on an island kingdom, a baby named Art was born. He was the only child of King and Queen Pendragon, but they were not a happy family. Soon after Art's birth, his parents separated and his mother moved away. They were not a happy kingdom either—war between the island clans plagued the region. At times arrows soared over the castle wall and battering rams thumped the gates. The king feared for the safety of his son, so baby Art was sent to live at a school called Merlin Hall. There, the staff were sworn to secrecy—told never to mention Art's lineage to keep him safe.

Separated from his family, King Pendragon grew despondent. The clan leaders were deeply embroiled in disputes and battles. Not a one listened to another, and no one listened to the king. Woe at work combined with heartbreak brought King Pendragon to an early death. With no heir to lead the kingdom, the country fell into despair.

Meanwhile, Art grew up at Merlin Hall in the care of warm people, garden-fresh food, music, art, and science. There were studies, outdoors sports, and friends to keep him busy. Yet Art's childhood wasn't entirely without sadness. His true parentage remained a mystery to him. No one visited on family day or sent cards or packages at birthdays or holidays. Sometimes Art would look in the mirror and study himself. He'd wonder what combination of people lived within him and who he would become.

Outside the school gates, the island remained at war. Sometimes the din of nearby battles would spill over into the school grounds and smoke from fires would darken the sky. When this happened, the students would retreat indoors and distract themselves by telling the legend of Merlin Hall.

The story told of the school's founding family and namesake, the Merlins. They were gifted oracles who could communicate with animals, command dragons, and bring a winter night's sky to life with color. The legend foretold that following King Pendragon's passing, the Merlins melted their magic staffs together with the late king's sword and sunk a new all-powerful sword into the stone cliffside where the school stood. An inscription on the sword read: "The one who draws this sword from stone, is right wise king of this great isle." Students scoured the campus with flash lights, but no one had ever found the sword.

As the years passed, Art's achievements at Merlin Hall were varied. Teachers noticed he was hard working and engaged. Yet he never raised his hand in class and was often quiet during discussions. He wasn't nominated to be a prefect, or a team captain when it came to sports. Art seemed rather unremarkable.

Then, one day during a picnic, a girl sat beside Art. Her face was red and her eyebrows poised like sparring caterpillars. She wiped a tear from her cheek and huffed, "My roommate took my sandwich and I'm furious." A broken lunchbox littered the ground nearby.

Art wanted to move away, but instead he did something surprising. He beckoned the girl's roommate over. "Tell me your side," he asked each child. Soon Art learned that the children were both worried about not having enough to eat. "Why didn't you tell someone?" Art asked softly.

"I'm not used to being listened to," one of the students confessed.

At that moment, a light went on in Art's head. He had always been good at listening. Perhaps this was his thing.

Art began to notice moments all around him where he could step in and help. When accusations of cheating were flung in a heated ball game, Art ran right into the fray, arms outstretched. "Can we talk about this?" he urged.

Art's outreach caught the attention of the headteacher. "I'd like you to head our student leadership council," she said one day. "You'll identify student leaders and show them how to be good listeners."

Art was astonished. "Why me?" he said. "I'm not anybody important."

But the headteacher raised a hand to halt him. "To help, I've paired you with a faculty liaison, Mr. Ambrosius."

Mr. Ambrosius was an older fellow with a triangular beard who just sort of grunted. For someone meant to help win over the students, Art thought Mr. Ambrosius was an odd choice. He lacked the posture and command that Art assumed a leader needed. That was until their first tutorial, when he saw butterflies and bees spring from Mr. Ambrosius's hands.

"Wow!" Art said. "You. . . you can do magic?"

"I used to conjure spells," Mr. Ambrosius said, his eyes glowing. "I helped knights on the battlefield. When they grew weary in battle, I brought a storm of hail upon their opponents. When the skies were filled with smoke and darkness, I summoned wolves to strike fear in the heart of the enemy."

Art was rapt. "But why can't you do that again, to stop all the battles?"

Mr. Ambrosius shook his head. "It was never enough. I learnt that no magic or might can cure discord between people. But don't be discouraged. There is something that can bring us peace."

"What is it?" Art asked, confused.

Mr. Ambrosius smiled. "I think you know, Art. Talking and listening. Through the student leadership council, we'll foster students poised to be wise and just rulers. It's your generation that will unite this land."

After that, little by little, week by week, Mr. Ambrosius and Art invited other students to share lessons such as: listening to an enemy, or how not to roll one's eyes or interrupt like a "know it all." And they worked together to coach one another on asking for help.

Mr. Ambrosius and Art invited the most promising students to be part of the student leadership council. They started with Lancelot, Gawain, Geri, and Percival. Then they added Lamorak, Kay, and Gareth who recommended Bedivere, Gaheris, and Galahad. After the mid-year break the group added Tristen and Pamaedes.

By then, they had outgrown their small study room and moved to the dining hall, which had a large, round table that better accommodated the growing group. There they met for many months and became known as the Junior Knights of Merlin Hall.

One day, as the school gathered for dinner, the bells in the Hall's tower rang without end. It was a signal that battle drew dangerously near and students must take cover. Teachers hurried younger students to safety through underground caves to awaiting boats. Older students worked with staff to fortify the school. Mr. Ambrosius called upon the Junior Knights to stay behind in the dining hall.

"How about staying to use your new skills?" Mr. Ambrosius said. "I believe you can succeed where others

have failed. This isn't a battle that will be won the old-fashioned way, this will be won with friendship!"

The Junior Knights looked from one to the other with worry. But Art stood and simply said, "I'm in."

The Junior Knights assembled on the roof to get the lay of the land. Beyond the school a great dust roiled, flames shot into the sky, and the glint of metal illuminated the battle which had drawn awfully close. It was loud with screams and shouts, rallying cries and drums, the neighing of horses, and the sound of metal striking metal.

The Junior Knights decided that during a break in the fighting they would go in pairs and coax leaders from the embattled clans to meet at a neutral place. "The clearing on the cliff ledge," Art called out. At twilight, his peers emerged from the woods and trails accompanied by battle-weary figures. Art invited each of them to sit cross-legged on the dirt so that everyone was an equal, and to describe their strife. As each leader told their tale, Art and the others listened for shared experiences and ways to help. This is what they heard:

"They stole our allotment," one leader accused.

"We want our forest back," another leader demanded.

"We want our logging access," another protested.

"We want the spring opened," a leader pushed.

"We want the spring dammed," another pressed back.

"We want the trade road restored." Some were now on their feet.

"We closed the road because it wasn't safe!" They got in one another's faces.

"You ruined our home," someone sobbed.

"No, you ruined our home," another wept.

No one was sure how an agreement could be reached. But to Art it sounded like the sports disputes he'd mediated at school, and he spoke up. "Tell me about your home, tell me about your clan. What do you love about them?"

And, like clouds parting after a storm, the leaders began to share.

"Our land has been home to our family of farmers for generations. There is nowhere more beautiful."

"Our village is serene and special, people share with one another and help their friends and neighbors."

"Our land has rivers filled with fish, which attract the most majestic birds."

"We teach our children to track those birds to show us new paths and trails."

And before everyone's eyes, the leaders began to huddle together. To draw pictures and maps in the dirt with their swords. They pulled items from pouches and showed them proudly. Then someone broke into a smile. Then another. And soon hands were being shook, chests bumped, backs patted with comradery. The Junior Knights took notes, relayed negotiations, and helped draft statements that the leaders could share with their people.

Mr. Ambrosius took Art aside. "What made you choose this spot for the meeting?" he asked. Art thought long and hard. He paced near the edge of the cliff nervously. "Something drew me here today," he said.

"Perhaps you should see why," Mr. Ambrosius said. He closed his eyes and the earth beneath them began to tremble. A huge crack forked beside Art and large sections of the cliff on either side broke loose, crashing into the sea. All that remained was a small spit upon which Art knelt, and an outlying piece of stone, on which shone the hilt of a mighty sword. The starlight illuminated the pommel like a ship's beacon. Everyone stared, mouths agape, at the mythic sword in the stone.

Mr. Ambrosius looked at Art and said gently, "I think you know what to do."

Art reached both hands forward, closed his eyes and gripped the hilt of the sword. Within him swirled the strangest concoction of purpose and place, knowing and unknowing, and the sensation of being home. As Art opened his eyes, the sword shot free from the stone, pulling Art's hands high into the air. And there on the edge of the cliff, surrounded by all the leaders in the land, Art was beheld as the new right wise king of the isle.

From that day forth, Art was known as King Arthur. Upon graduating from Merlin Hall, he began his work. It was a big job, not to be done alone. So, Art brought in a council of leaders to represent all the different clans in the kingdom. And who did he choose for those all-important roles? None other than his trusted school friends, the Junior Knights. He even had their old table from Merlin Hall put in his study. It was there, at the round table with room enough for all, that they began every gathering with a salute to their mentor and friend, Mr. Ambrosius Merlin.

Art was beheld as the new right wise king of the isle.

Tom Thumb

Once upon a time, on a forested mountain top, there lived a couple of lumberjacks. They worked night and day to buy a small plot of land that no one else wanted. The people in the nearest city thought they were strange and never stopped by or invited them into town. "Mountain people are all a bit odd," they'd say. "You never know what they are doing up there. It's not normal to live with only trees for company."

The couple were often blamed for things by the villagers for no good reason. When the maple syrup ran out, the villagers blamed the mountain couple. When the stream ran low, they blamed the mountain couple. They would stare at the couple when they made lumber deliveries to the mill with their homemade horse trailer.

So, the couple got by all on their own with very little. So little in fact that holes went unpatched in their house and, with no market-sellers stopping their way, they often went without fresh food. Though the two wished for a child, they never felt able to have one, for they could scarcely keep a roof over their own heads. But as they worked, unknown to them, some fairies called Forest Sprites scampered nearby. They heard the couple's wishes and took it upon themselves to grant them.

One day, the couple returned home after a hard day's work and were greeted with a staggering surprise. Their home had a shiny new roof and a fresh coat of paint. A new spring ran clear where an old well once stood, and a new wood stove resided at the heart of the cozy home.

That evening, the couple warmed themselves by the fire and admired their new home improvements. "This will last us well into our old age!" marveled the woman.

"The smallest changes make all the difference," said the man as he stoked the fire.

"Nothing is too small to be meaningful," said the woman, not knowing how true her words were.

The couple retired for the night, but were awoken in the wee hours by the sound of humming. They peered apprehensively through their bedroom key hole into the living room. There, leaning against the ottoman, stood a young man, not even tall enough to reach the top of the foot stool cushion.

The two nearly fell through the door with surprise.

"Can we help you?" the woman asked.

"Oh golly no," said the small guest. "I am here to help you! I was sent by the Forest Sprites."

The lumberjacks were overjoyed. They quickly

made the young fellow feel welcome. "Do you have a name?" asked the man as he gathered a warm drink in an acorn cap for the young visitor.

"I do not, perhaps you'd like to give me one?"

"Shall we name you Tom after my father?" the woman asked.

Their new charge nodded happily.

"Why, you're not much bigger than the thumb of a grizzly!" noted the man. "How about we call you Tom Thumb?" And the three sealed it with a hug.

As the years passed, Tom and his new family grew in closeness and comfort. Tom worked hard to learn every bit of the family trade. Even though he was an unusual size, he was skilled and thoughtful. He patiently took in his mother's instructions for felling trees, pruning, and climbing, as well as his father's techniques for measuring, coring, sampling, and tapping. After pondering a task, he would come up with a clever accommodation to allow him to perform just as a full-size person would.

When it came to riding horses, Tom made an amazing discovery. He set up a washboard at the horse's flank, scaled his way to the horse's mane, and pulled himself aboard. Instead of using reins, he hopped on to the horse's head and spoke directly in its ear. Before his parents' eyes the horse trotted around in a little parade.

"Now I can take wood to town!" he proclaimed proudly.

His parents weren't sure. "You'll need to be extra careful. People are not always welcoming to people who are different," cautioned Tom's mother.

But Tom was determined. The next morning off he went with a small load of lumber. As Tom neared the market, a patrolman barricaded him from entering the walls of the city. "Show yourself, rider!" he boomed.

"I'm just here," piped Tom from behind the horse's ear. The patrolman leaned in to inspect him.

"Why, you're not much bigger than a thumb. Up to no good, I presume?"

"I'm off to the mill to deliver this load of lumber," Tom protested.

"Hmmm," muttered the patrolman. "Well, be on your way, but I've got my eye on you."

Inside the walls, Tom found the city was bursting with fun. There were musicians

and performers, a puppet stage and food vendors. Animals roamed free, food was for sale, and there was even a table with games.

As Tom went about his business, on the outskirts of the city lurked a dangerous element. A band of robbers had beset the place. Dressed in fancy costumes with knee-high socks they combed the crowd; picking coins from pockets and helping themselves to snacks from unattended market stalls.

The leader of the group spotted a shiny collection of coins at the bottom of a cellar beside the old mill. "Psst!" one robber said to another. "This must be the city treasury!" The robbers tried their best to remove the iron grate that covered the opening to the cellar, but it was impossible.

As Tom went to collect his horse to return home, he noticed them peering into the cellar. "Can I help you with something?" he asked.

The robbers turned around and searched for the sound of the voice.

"Hey, this horse talks!" exclaimed one of them.

"Nah, you goof, it's this little chap," stated the last one. His gaze landed on Tom. "Why don't you buzz off, we certainly don't need a little shrimp like you underfoot."

Tom turned to scale the side of the mill and climb atop his horse.

"Wait just a second there, little friend . . ." said the first robber, noticing Tom's size and skill. I think we could use your help. We . . . uh . . . dropped all our earnings from the market down this cellar. You think you could help us get it if we were to lower you down?" The robber gestured beneath the iron grate to the darkness below.

"Oh how unfortunate," said Tom. "I'd be glad to lend a hand." And soon enough, Tom found himself tethered to a rope made from the gang's stinky socks, lowered through the iron grate and into the depths of the cellar.

"I see it," Tom cried. "I see the coins!"

The robbers shared greedy grins. "Tie the bag to your waist and we'll haul you up," they instructed.

Tom did as he was told and the crew yanked him back up to the top.

"Oh, wow, you're speedy," Tom remarked as the robbers hastily untied him. While Tom scrambled atop his horse, the robbers busied themselves with counting 'their' money. One glanced his way. "Hold on there, before you go, here's a small piece for your help," he said and tossed Tom a small gold coin. "Now to the inn!" the robber said. "I'll buy the drinks!"

When Tom returned home that evening, his parents were already asleep. He crept in quietly and tucked the shiny gold piece into a cookie jar, thinking he'd surprise everyone in the morning.

But in the morning, Tom slept in. And when his mother heard a knock at the door she was greeted with a different sort of surprise. An imposing patrolman, helmet in hand and sword by his side, stood on the threshold.

Tom did as he was told and the crew yanked him back up to the top.

"My goodness, can I help you with something?" Tom's mother stammered.

"We are seeking a band of robbers who raided the city treasury yesterday," the patrolman explained. "Have you seen any suspicious characters around, Ma'am?"

"Whatever do you mean?" asked Tom's father, joining the pair at the door. "What does 'suspicious' look like?"

The patrolman was surprised. "Someone out of the ordinary, someone different from the folks we have in the city."

"We welcome strangers on our land. We don't look down on difference," Tom's mom stated proudly.

The patrolman looked taken aback. "Well, I didn't mean to offend."

"Apology accepted. Won't you have a cookie on your way?" Tom's dad offered the cookie jar so the patrolmen could select a treat. "So there's no hard feelings."

"Well, don't mind if I do," the patrolman said and reached in the jar. Only instead of a cookie the patrolman pulled out the gold piece!

The patrolman's expression soured as he inspected it. "This is marked with the seal of the city. How did you come by this? It's part of the stolen loot."

The couple looked stunned. "We've no idea how that got there," they pleaded, but the patrolman arrested them on the spot and tied them to a tree. The commotion roused Tom from his sleep and he raced out in his jammies. "What is the meaning of this? Let them go!" Tom cried.

"These two have stolen from the city treasury," the patrolmen said, ready to leave for the town jail. "Looking around this old place with a shiny new roof and stove, I wager they spent the contraband already! This gold coin is all that's left." The patrolman held up the gold piece.

Tom's eyes widened as he took in the evidence. "I know just where that came from. I can take you to the people who took it."

Tom leapt from stump to stump, then from limb to limb, and reached the shoulders of the patrolman's steed. He whispered in its ear and the horse was off like a shot, bounding down the road towards the city.

Outside the city was an inn that greeted travelers. Tom asked the horse to stop and he slid down its mane.

"Inside the inn you'll find the real robbers," he said.

And sure enough, when the patrolman and Tom entered the inn, they found the robbers in knee-high socks sleeping at a lonely table littered with empty dishes. When they snored, their bodies jingled with the sound of loose coins.

Tom and the patrolman shook the thieves awake and an abundance of coins fell to the floor. The patrolman was shocked and called for the inspector. While they secured the true culprits and recovered the city treasure, Tom returned and untied his parents.

"I can't believe they thought you were mixed up in this." Tom was in tears. "I'm so sorry!"

"Sometimes that happens," Tom's mother consoled him. "People take one look at your life and decide something about you that is not true."

"But it's all my fault, if I hadn't been so eager to help . . ." Tom started.

"Oh, don't ever lose your desire to help others. It's what saved us today," his father comforted.

The following day, Tom and his family received a knock on the door. It was the inspector!

"Sorry to bother you," he began. "I wanted to offer you an official apology from our office. We were wrong to make assumptions about you lumberjacks."

The family welcomed him in and this time there were cookies—and only cookies—in the cookie jar. Over a sweet treat the foursome talked, and the inspector proposed an idea. "How'd you like to be the Forest Warden for the mountains, Tom? We need an ambassador who understands the important work of this community. It would help to keep us connected and prevent mistakes like the wrongful accusation you experienced. Whatd'ya say?"

"I say yes!" Tom chimed in.

Tom received a special uniform with a badge and belt, and a very tall hat so all could spot him. He welcomed members of the police from all over the region to the mountain top to learn from and build relationships with each other. The connections built at Tom's mountain retreats shaped officers who were just and understanding. So Tom's legacy became more than just the thoughtful care of the forest. It became the thoughtful treatment of people.

Hercules

Long ago, in a land beside a clear blue sea, was born a boy named Hercules. He was the son of the king, but his mother was a commoner. At the time of his birth, his father was in fact married to someone else. Her name was Hera and she was a great warrior. She wasn't exactly eager to spend time raising the youngster. Irritated, Hera dropped magical serpents into Hercules' cradle. She hoped they might bite him so he would get sick and be sent away. Instead, baby Hercules hugged the serpents and they licked his face playfully. Seeing Hercules' command of the snakes, an idea arrived in Hera's head. She decided to embrace her role as stepmother on one condition: that the baby follow in her footsteps and become a noted warrior. "I'll include him in our family so long as I can put my mark on him!" Hera proclaimed. The king granted her request.

From that moment on, Hera raised young Hercules to be her replica. "He must be strong and brave, a slayer of beasts!" she declared. Her dream was closer than she could have imagined. For the snakes that had licked baby Hercules made him stronger and mightier than anyone who had come before him.

As Hercules grew, Hera called upon the best teachers to teach him wrestling, horseback riding, fencing, archery, and chariot driving. He even learned to play the lyre (a cool old harp). Hercules excelled in everything and Hera rewarded him with praise. "You're the strongest boy out there," she said, slapping him on the back as they looked out over their kingdom. He was pleased to win the affection of his stepmother and it inspired him to work hard.

Hercules effortlessly grew to be a star warrior. While everyone else was exhausted, worn out, and bruised, Hercules protected the kingdom from rivals and monsters with ease. His compatriots were wowed, and Hera beamed. She had statues erected in his image and a portrait commissioned to hang as a banner at the city gates.

Hercules, however, was embarrassed. When people recognized him from the banner, they'd stare and whistle at him. "Hey, Herc, break this log over my head?" they'd say. When people encountered the statue of him, they'd pose alongside it in silly ways or pretend they were fighting with him. Hercules also grew tired of Hera's one-sided affection. She only liked one thing about him, the warrior stuff. But that

was only part of who he really was. When no one was looking, Hercules could often be found reading quietly outside the hospital. One day, a doctor saw him. "If you are just sitting around, I could use a hand in here," she said. Hercules looked around for Hera and, not seeing her, slipped into the tent.

Inside, he was surrounded by neat rows of beds. Beside each stood highly organized care teams of doctors, nurses, and assistants attending to people's needs. The doctor asked him to move some equipment. Hercules nodded politely. It was nice to be needed by someone other than Hera. After that, whenever he could sneak away from Hera's watchful eye he would lend a hand at the hospital building beds, lifting loads, and getting to know the interesting patients and care providers. Sometimes it was sad, as when he heard a patient draw a final breath. But other times it was rewarding, like when a child with an injured leg was able to walk again. He was fascinated.

Hera soon noticed all the time he was spending at the hospital. She was unimpressed. "I can't have our greatest weapon and my apprentice wasting away in the healing arts," she muttered. Hera thought hard and then summoned Hercules to a meeting.

"I've a proposal for you," Hera laid out. "I've noticed that your mind's been elsewhere recently, so I've created a list of challenging labors to help you refocus."

Hercules was crestfallen. The list began like this:

1. Kill the notorious Namean Lion, who is resistant to weapons.
2. Kill the Hydra, a venomous beast with nine heads.
3. Catch the deer with the golden antlers.
4. Capture a majestic boar.
5. Clean dirty stables belonging to the cavalry horses in just a day . . .

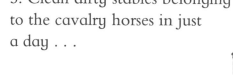

On and on it went, ending with the theft of a dog named Cerberus said to have three heads! Kill this, capture that, these were all things Hera thought were important. And they didn't appeal to Hercules at all.

"The thing is," Hercules said, taking a deep breath, "being a warrior isn't what I want to do. I've been volunteering, and I was thinking I'd like to learn more about healing and less about hurting."

"Absolutely not," Hera said. "You are the greatest fighter in the land. Plus, you wouldn't want to let me down, would you?"

Heavy-hearted, Hercules returned to his room, gathered his things and set off that evening. Soon he arrived at the den of the Namean Lion: a fearsome beast with a big ratty mane, a mouth of serrated teeth, and massive sword-like claws. Hercules knew he couldn't fight the beast with weapons, so he challenged the creature to a round of hand-to-hand combat.

The lion accepted and rose up on its feet. The two jumped into the throes of wrestling, rolling on the floor, holding each other's bodies, moving together like a great ball of rope. Hercules was a skillful wrestler and soon won the fight. He pressed against the lion's neck and the animal drew close to its last breath. At the last moment, Hercules removed his hand. The lion gasped for air. Hercules reached out a hand to help the animal up.

"Thank you," the lion panted. "You could have bested me, why did you stop?"

Hercules thought about it. "Your loss of breath, it reminded me of something," he reflected, thinking of his time in the hospital.

"For sparing my life, I'd like to give you the gift of my mane," the lion said. It took its sharp claws and trimmed the fur around its face, then handed the mane to Hercules, who took it gratefully.

Hercules then went off in search of the Hydra. He wondered to himself about the strange encounter with the lion. Why had he paused? But soon his thoughts were interrupted, for he could see in the distance the fantastic monster. It did indeed have nine heads and they were all deep in conversation.

Hercules shot an

arrow high in the sky to get the creature's attention. The heads all talked at once as they watched the arrow sail toward them. "Move to the left!" one head cried out. "No move to the right," shouted another. "Whose right, mine or yours?" asked another head. "Duck!" yelled another head. "I'll pass on duck, thank you, I'm more of chicken eater myself," a head babbled. "Incoming!" cried one last head as it took the arrow right in the neck. "Ouch."

Hercules raced beside the Hydra. The head that took the arrow disappeared in a puff of smoke. Then Hercules watched, eyes wide, as two new heads appeared where the injured head had once been. "Whoa," he exclaimed. "You heal yourself, don't you?"

The new heads coughed and cleared their throats. "Why, yes, of course we do. That is the way of the Hydra."

"What a miracle," said Hercules. "I don't want to harm you."

"We are so grateful. Please keep the arrow as a souvenir of our meeting," offered the Hydra. Hercules lifted the arrow which dripped with mysterious iridescent blue blood. "It carries our healing powers," the Hydra said as it bowed and slipped away.

Hercules should have raced off to his next labor. But his feet stayed put. What he had just witnessed held him in his path. "I can defeat a fierce lion, but would rather not," he thought aloud. "I could slay a monster but to what end? It might hold a healing miracle!" He stood, arrow in hand, and made a brave decision. With his mind made up, he raced back to confront Hera.

Hercules spotted Hera on a balcony.

"Finished already?" she said suspiciously.

"Yes!" Hercules called up. "All this time everyone thought I was so brave, but I was not. I couldn't stand up to you. Being a warrior is your thing, not mine. I quit."

Hera did not take the news well. She strode down from the porch, ripped the banners with Hercules' face from the gates and stormed out of the palace. "If you're not able to finish this, I will!" she seethed. And off she went into the setting sun.

Hera raged through the countryside. She captured the golden deer at first light. She plucked the majestic bull right from the kingdom of the centaurs before they were back from breakfast. At lunchtime she rode into the cavalry stables and frightened them into tidying up. On and on she went. She drove away birds from the fields, took the horns off a massive bull that she scared out of the sea and, just to show off, she stopped over at the island of the Amazons and made off with one of their famed jeweled belts.

Meanwhile, Hercules had secured himself a post at the hospital. He proved an eager student at the side of the doctors and nurses who worked there. They showed him how to keep patients comfortable, how to clean and dress wounds, record data, and keep charts. He learned how to recognize common ailments and how to prepare patients for surgery.

Then one day the hospital received word of a warrior in distress. Doctors and nurses raced to the rescue. "What is it? Can I help?" Hercules offered. "Someone's tried to capture a three-headed dog!" a nurse called back.

Hercules immediately knew the warrior in distress was Hera. "Wait, I'll come with you!" Hercules jumped onto the back of the moving chariot and off they raced.

Arriving on the scene, the medical team found Hera trapped beneath the massive three-headed dog. Hercules could see that the dog needed to be moved in order to treat Hera. He gently approached the creature then took the lion's mane from around his own neck and wrapped it round the animal like a sling. Hercules gave the dog a gentle roll onto its feet and it lumbered away, revealing Hera with a wound in her neck. The team got right to assessing the patient, and found her injuries were too severe to move her. The mood among the group changed from hopeful to grim. Hercules, however, remembered the Hydra. He withdrew the arrow and gently applied some of the iridescent blue goo from the point to Hera's wound. Before everyone's eyes, she began to heal. Soon Hera was well enough to be moved to the hospital.

On the chariot ride back, Hercules sat beside Hera and held her hand. Her eyes opened, and she smiled, grateful to be in his care. "I think you are right my boy. The hospital is where you need to be."

"I'd like that," Hercules said quietly. "You be the warrior, leave the care and repair to me."

When Hera recovered, she replaced the statue of Hercules with one showing a snake circling a column; a symbol of the strength, diversity, and stability that held up not only their family, but their community. Hercules was touched and added the symbol to his nurse's uniform, so he could always remember that he had the support of his family in his work. He remained the first face of care for so many, from the hospital to the battlefield. From then on, the only time his mighty arms were the talk of the town was when they gently cradled a newborn baby.

On the chariot ride back, Hercules sat beside Hera and held her hand.

Sinbad

Once, beside a green sea, lay a dazzling city carved of white stone. Its rooftops were punctuated with golden domes and spires, and from the narrow-cobbled streets climbed fragrant smoke, laughter, and the voices of thousands of people. The stone city was made up of two distinct worlds. One was of grand residences, with lush courtyards and towering rooms decked with mirrored lanterns for entertaining. The second world lay beneath this one: on the street level, where the cooks, housekeepers, helping hands, gardeners, fisher folk, and butlers resided. In each part of the city, there lived a man named Sinbad. The two lived nearly side by side but never met.

Until one day, when both Sinbads went to the same sandwich stand—Salty's Surf, a beach kiosk with stools in the sand. One Sinbad, a stately fellow with beads in his long white hair, ordered eggplant fritters with sesame sauce. The other Sinbad, a young man with a sun streaked bun and a worn backpack, ordered boiled egg with sesame sauce. When chef Salty called out "Sinbad!" the two men both stepped up to grab their food, mistakenly getting each other's order.

"Chef, this looks delicious, but I didn't order eggs," said the first Sinbad.

"I think this must be yours," the younger Sinbad replied, handing him his fritters.

"Thank you! Are you also called Sinbad?" the elder gentleman asked, biting into his lunch.

"Yes, I am. But my friends call me Bab. I have never met anyone of the same name. Are you from these parts?"

"That's a long story," the elder Sinbad said as he pulled out a couple of beach stools. "I was a sailor, so I come from many places. When I was your age, I made a living through trickery and games, gambling, and cons. I cheated the wrong people and there was a bounty on my head, so I had to flee. I snuck onto a merchant vessel called *The Genie* and set sail for my future!"

"What a coincidence that we should meet," said Bab. "I've just been granted a post as a merchant marine on a ship called the *Scarab*. I depart next month and I am terribly nervous. What should I expect?"

"Expect the unexpected, my friend," Sinbad said, then launched into a tale:

"No sooner had we set sail when we encountered a storm. The boat heaved from side to side and soon water rained down on me from the cabin doors and portholes. On deck the crew raced and screamed. I can't recall which was louder—the wind, the rain, the cries of the sailors, or the commands of the captain. I trembled in my hiding spot until the roil of the ship was so great, I passed out from fear!"

Bab looked freaked out. "Is this supposed to ease my nerves?" he asked with a tense laugh.

"I came to and found myself lying on a sandy beach," Sinbad continued, not realizing he was worrying his listener. "A few crew members had weathered the storm with me and we gathered to make a fire to dry ourselves. Just as the kindling caught and smoke began to tinge the air, we felt a great stirring beneath our feet."

Sinbad rose from his stool to act out the next part of the story.

"The beach began to shudder and fall away, and right where we stood rose a vast gray stone. We clung to one another, we fell to our knees! For the island was no island at all, but a majestic whale!"

Sinbad grinned ear to ear but Bab shook his head with shock. "I don't know if you've eased my mind or made me more afraid," he confessed. "What happened next? How did you get to safety?"

"The great creature opened its massive mouth full of bristly teeth and spat out our ship! We swam for our lives, scrambled aboard and got out of there as quickly as we could. But it was nothing compared to what happened next. Meet me here this time next week and I'll tell you all about it!"

Bab was nervous to hear the rest, but a week later he went to Salty's Surf again.

"It all started when *The Genie* discovered a foggy lagoon," Sinbad said over a chickpea platter. "We happened upon it by chance, drawn there by the strangest song I ever heard, like a silken bow against the smoothest shell. . ."

"Don't tell me, sirens? Those aren't real, right?" Bab asked with worry in his voice.

"They are real! But have no fear, my friend, they don't devour the souls of sailors like myths suggest. They retrieve sunken ships and heal ailing mariners. They helped us find our way back, their song putting joyful memories in place of scary shipwreck ones."

"Wow," Bab gulped. "You are awfully brave—a storm, a whale, a siren's song. What could top that?"

"Let's dine again next week," Sinbad said with a wink.

For many weeks, Bab met Sinbad for lunch and stories, hoping to ready himself for his journey ahead. Sinbad told of magic lamps that granted wishes, of mirages in the desert with pools of jewels and trees ripe with fruits. The story that captivated Bab the most was of an enormous bird. At first it had frightened Sinbad and his crewmates, but in their hour of need it rescued them from a band of pirates, sweeping down to pluck them from a cliff's edge in the nick of time.

Throughout the stories Bab listened attentively. However, as time went on, he started to worry about his decision to set sail. The stories Sinbad told were exciting, but they were also frightening.

When Bab's big day arrived, chef Salty threw the Sinbads a free lunch with bunting and balloons. The ship on which Bab was listed—the *Scarab*—waited just in view, flag flying high. Sinbad arrived early, his captain's hat in hand, eager to see off his young friend.

The noon sun beat down on the eatery and lunch patrons came and went, but none were Bab. Then the sun lowered in the afternoon sky and visitors came for cold drinks and iced sweets. By early evening, there was still no sign of Bab.

"Where could he be?" Sinbad murmured to chef Salty.

"You tell me. I thought you knew him well," Salty replied as he closed up shop. "His ship departs this evening. Why don't you ask the captain?"

Sinbad strode over to the *Scarab* and called up to the deck. The captain came into view, holding the manifest and checking the list of names. "I'm holding the ship for a new sailor named Sinbad," she called over. "Do you happen to be him?"

"No, but he's my friend. I'm having trouble finding him myself," Sinbad confessed.

"What does he look like?" the captain probed.

"I never really noticed."

"Where does he live?" she asked.

"I never inquired!" Sinbad admitted, alarmed by his own disregard.

Distressed, Sinbad hurried back into town. How had he been so foolish? While he'd told stories each week, he'd scarcely asked young Bab a single question. Or helped to quell his fear of his sea voyage. The poor fellow might have given up the most exciting opportunity of his life!

Sinbad knocked on doors frantically. "Have you seen a young sailor?" he begged at each door. "They call him Bab!"

After some time, he landed on a helpful doorstep. "Why yes, I know Bab," a young woman said. "He lives near the park."

"Oh, I live near the park!" exclaimed Sinbad and he raced to his own street. He rang his neighbors' doorbells but to no avail. Defeated, he sat on a park bench and looked at the grand homes that lined the fine park. Peacocks settled on the stone walls for the night and lights began to come on in the windows.

That was when Sinbad took notice of his street from a new perspective. Not only had lights appeared upstairs in the grand homes, but they were warming the windows below the street too. There was a whole other set of doors he hadn't thought to try. He started with the one across from his home. He smoothed back his hair, straightened his clothes, and descended the stairs to the entrance. He raised his hand to knock when the door opened by surprise.

There on the threshold stood Bab. He looked ragged and forlorn.

"My friend, I've been looking for you. Today is your big day!" Sinbad bellowed. "Where have you been?"

"I've decided to decline my post," Bab said, stepping out into the night. "I listened carefully to your stories and I see now that I'm not sailing material."

"Oh no!" Sinbad gasped and stepped back. "I . . . I meant to inspire you, not discourage you."

"It's not your fault. If you knew me better, you'd know I have a lot of fears," Bab admitted. "I'm a nervous guy."

"Yeah, I guess we don't really know one another at all. All those lunches we had, I mostly just carried on, didn't I?" Sinbad said.

Bab nodded in agreement. "It's OK. I got kind of swept away in your tales. No one from this part of the city has ever been a merchant marine."

Sinbad got quiet. "Truth is, I was really scared on my first voyage."

"You were?!" Bab looked to his hero.

"You bet," Sinbad admitted. "Sailing isn't all high-seas adventure, full of magic and miracles. It's hard work, for hours on end, forging trusting friendships and learning to be a leader. That's how you'll know what to do when an adventure comes your way. Seafaring is perfect for someone as sensitive as yourself."

A smile broke across Bab's face. "You really think I can do it?" he said, accepting Sinbad's hand.

"I do," Sinbad said as the two strode back to the harbor. "Plus, this old sea dog might have one last journey in him . . ." Sinbad secured his captain's hat upon his head.

Under the stars and a luminous moon, the *Scarab* eased out of the harbor. Aboard the ship, Sinbad saw to it that Bab had the best experience at sea. He helped the young sailor pick out a central sleeping hammock to stave off sea-sickness. In the morning, he helped Bab and the other new sailors' practise their knots. In the evening, they studied star navigation as a group.

The crew of the *Scarab* sailed far and wide. Sinbad, Bab, and the crew met all kinds of people and visited a great many places. The seas were kind to them, and they were kind to those they met along the way. Once in a tight lagoon, Bab saw the shadow of a great bird shade the deck. The hairs on the back of his head stood up, but he remembered the stories of Sinbad and bravely stayed the course. The bird, it turned out, needed only a guide, and the lights of the *Scarab* led the creature back out to sea. Another time, on a moonless night, Bab and the crew heard a Siren's song. The crew followed the solemn ballad, and avoided a dangerous reef known for shipwrecks. And on one particular voyage, a dark island caught Bab's eye, it so resembled a whale. He pointed to the gray mass and called out with joy, "Sails up team, adventure awaits!"

But what happened next is a matter for another story entirely.

"Sails up team, adventure awaits!"

The Emperor's New Clothes

Once upon a time, in the heart of an empire that spanned mountains and seas, sat an enormous palace. Inside the palace lived an enormously important family: Emperor On and his son Piào.

Emperor On was a reserved fellow. He believed that there was a place for everything and everything had a place, and this included clothes. Uniforms were strictly abided by and he himself dressed in austere tunics and robes, neutral shoes and not an inch of jewelry.

On's son Piào was different. He dressed in bright silks layered with fur and sheep skins. He accessorized with leather pouches, hats, and boots with colored laces. His outward appearance was an extension of his warm and lively personality. He was eager to help others and brighten the world around him. However, Piào's efforts did not go over well at court. Some of the murmurs that passed through the palace when Piào strode by were: "Wow, I've never seen feathers worn like that before!" or "Is that meant to be a top? It looks more like a beach umbrella!" followed by snickers or sideways glances.

Piào's toughest critic was his father. Emperor On cautioned his son that when he was emperor, he would be expected to tone down his playful wardrobe. "You do know you'll need to start dressing like a leader? The people will look to you as an example, they'll need continuity to feel safe!" he warned, looking at Piào's collection of jewelry.

One day, the emperor set off on a perilous journey into the mountain mines. Sadly, the trip went awry and the elder leader never returned. Under a cloud of sadness young Piào took the throne.

Piào fretted over what to wear for his coronation. He could hear the final quarrel he'd had with his father echoing in his head, pleading him to follow in his footsteps. As the countdown to the big day neared Piào tried on everything in his closet. He needed his people to know he was confident, capable, and steadfast; honest, genuine, and true. But when Piào turned to the mirror, no matter what he was wearing, he saw only his father's doubt. Seeking help, he turned to Noble Li, his imperial advisor. "Send out a summons for all royal weavers and designers of the region," Piào decreed. "I'm seeking a true artisan to create my coronation outfit!"

Weavers and designers poured in from all over the empire. They modeled finery for Piào that normally would have spoken to him. But Piào believed he needed to change his look to win the approval of the court, so one by one, he sent them away. Just as the doors were closing, a brother and sister who had overheard the day's affairs slipped in. Unfortunately, they were not weavers, but con artists. The two had hatched a plan to take advantage of the young emperor and they began to thread the needle of their scam.

"We can help your royal highness, we dabble in the obscure textile arts," they explained. "We can make you a fine suit that will magically permit you to see if you've earned the admiration of your citizens. Only those loyal and true will be able to see its splendor. They will shower you with praise! To everyone else, the doubters and naysayers, well, they won't see anything at all. The clothes will be invisible."

They bowed low, wondering if Piào would see through their scheme, but Piào hadn't even listened to the end. "An outfit that shows whether my people approve of me?" he said in wonder. "How wonderful!"

"All we require is accommodation," the sister said smoothly, "for the work takes place day and night."

"And a chest of gold bars for materials, and a bag of rare gems for the ribbons and trimmings," her brother added.

Piào agreed and the two troublemakers moved into the imperial palace at once. They requested that a bold placard be placed outside their door to explain the delicate nature of their work. It read: *Magical Textiles Studio: exclusive viewing for loyal and true subjects only.* In small print below, it read: *If you can't readily appreciate the charmed fashion, see the information desk regarding exile and relocation planning.*

As they worked, Piào sent different members of the court to check on the progress. First Noble Li went to see the materials. He took in the sign at the door. "Whatever could that mean?" he thought to himself. But when he opened the door, he began to understand. The brother and sister were seated at the work table, scissors in hand, cutting out a pattern. Yet, when they pulled the paper stencil away, there was ZERO upon the table. Not a thread, scrap, or a ball of fuzz, nothing!

"Well, what do you think?" grinned the siblings. "Isn't it just lustrous?" The brother closed his eyes and stroked the "material."

Noble Li thought he might barf. Was he not loyal and true? No one was more so than he! "It's stunning," he fibbed, hurrying away.

Full of worry, Noble Li sent the imperial librarian to see the garments too. She was a learned person. "Surely she will see the artists' vision," thought Noble Li. But when the librarian entered, she took in a strange scene.

"Hi, just in time to see us dressing the model!" the brother said.

"I just LOVE the drape!" the sister bragged. "The lines are so innovative, don't you think?"

The librarian was careful not to let her alarm show on her face, since all she saw were hundreds of pins puncturing a bare mannequin. She knew if she were to remain on the imperial staff she must say the right thing. "It's unlike anything I've seen before," she hurried. "I'll be sure to include it in the archive."

Day after day, different members of the imperial staff visited the design shop. Day after day, they saw the brother and sister stitching, fastening, pressing, and steaming what looked like nothing at all. But when they read the entry placard they were reminded of how important the garments were, and immediately praised their glamour and look (which they entirely could not see!).

The big day arrived, and the young emperor gathered his team. The designer duo dressed the new leader in his finery with ceremony and exaggerated gestures. It was an elaborate pantomime, because the brother and sister hadn't done a stitch of work. It had all been an elegant fraud. There was nothing to dress the emperor with, not even underwear. He would be parading in the buff!

But the emperor seemed unfazed. Noble Li oohed and aaahed, and suggested a portrait be commissioned. The librarian stifled a laugh, but then quickly covered it with applause. So, young Piào was under the impression everyone greatly approved of his stunning new outfit. He strode from his dressing room and out into the grounds without so much as a glance in the mirror.

Assembled on the palace promenade stood all the citizens of the land, eager to receive their

"How could I be such a fool?" Piáo asked himself.

leader. As the nude emperor splashed into the sunlight, a collective gasp flew up from the crowd. Piào took it as affirmation, and walked proudly along the pathways, past hundreds of wide eyes and gaping mouths.

"I thought he liked dressing up. What happened?" someone whispered.

"I knew we were getting a young emperor, but this is a little too fresh," another murmured.

"I can't be the only one seeing this?" a third muttered.

Only one little child dared to speak out. "Your highness, I think you are very brave to parade around without any clothes!"

The crowd fell painfully still. The emperor stopped. No one dared look him in the eye, except for the little child, who stepped forward and stretched out their scarf to offer Piào some concealment. Then the child led Piào to a fountain to find his reflection. "How could I be such a fool?!" Piào asked himself, embarrassed tears stinging the edges of his eyes as he hurried back to the comfort of his room.

A while later, Noble Li knocked on the door. "I'm so sorry, my young Emperor. I failed you."

"It's OK," Piào said gloomily. "I let myself be led astray by those troublemakers. I just wanted everyone to approve of me so much."

"Might I suggest how we can fix this?" Noble Li said. He walked to the closet and opened the door.

Emperor Piào lit up as he saw his treasured fashions inside. Noble Li was right. He needed to reconnect with his true self. The person whose clothing could tell a story about what he held dear. He selected a pair of trousers painted with a pastoral scene to honor the farmland of his empire. A blouse bedecked with fish to celebrate the water-faring people of his land. A leather jacket to show his pride for the ranchers of the deserts. Lastly, Piào added a cap as red as the rubies from the mountain mines where his father last stood. The new look showed the emperor's thoughtful spirit, pride in his people, and respect for the past.

"Now the people can truly meet their leader," he said to himself, looking in the mirror.

Noble Li reassembled the citizens for the parade. Piào invited the brave child who had helped him to be his attendant along the boulevard. "I've a big announcement to make and I need your help," he told the child, and gave them the special job of holding the train of a great cape he concealed his outfit in.

"Assembled citizens," Piào announced, "forgive my earlier error. I misunderstood my father's last lesson for me. That to be worthy of your respect, I must above all

respect myself. If I'm to earn the trust of a nation, I must trust you with my greatest asset, the real me."

The child then pulled back the cape to reveal Piào's self-styled coronation regalia. It was a triumph surpassed only by his smile of joy.

In the years that followed, Piào got his footing as emperor and made a few changes around the palace. Uniforms went by the wayside and everyone was encouraged to dress as they liked. The brother and sister con artists were apprehended trying to spend their gold bricks in the imperial village and were sentenced to rake the sands at the nudist beach.

Emperor Piào expanded the design studio into a space for actual designers where they could take risks and showcase their work. His favorite addition was an annual youth fashion show. Children from all over the kingdom submitted creative designs and the emperor would have them custom-made and modeled by volunteers who could be anyone from bakers to barbers, ranch hands to royals. Everyone had a fashion story to tell—and as for the emperor, the kingdom was forever his muse.

Pinocchio

Once upon a time, in a quaint village, there lived a carpenter named Geppetto. He had no family, few possessions and though his tools kept him company he was often lonely. One winter evening, as flakes of snow began to fall, he found himself absent-mindedly carving a log to reveal a friendly face. It amused him, and he continued to work until a puppet emerged from the wood. He sat the character upon his bench, crawled into bed, and fell fast asleep.

While Geppetto slept, his workshop was visited by a magical Blue Fairy. With a wave of his wand, the puppet wriggled and leaped upon the work-bench with glee.

"I'm alive, a real boy!" the puppet cried with a grin on his face.

"Not so fast, little friend," the Blue Fairy interrupted. "You might feel like a real boy, but your heart is still made of wood."

"But I want the heart of a real boy," the puppet complained. "How can I get it?"

"That you'll have to learn on your own," supplied the Blue Fairy with a smile. "But I'll leave you with a guide to help you on your way."

He disappeared with a sparkle and a little cricket named Cinguettio appeared in his place. "I'll be right here beside you," Cinguettio said, perching on Pinocchio's shoulder. "If you ever need help, just ask."

"Ha! I don't need any help," scoffed Pinocchio, bouncing and springing around the small home. This, of course, woke Geppetto.

"Who are you?" he said, astonished.

"You tell me!" the puppet grinned.

Geppetto picked up the puppet and inspected him carefully, delighted to have someone to share his home with. "I'll call you Pinocchio!" he exclaimed, hugging his new family member.

"And I'll call you Papa!" said Pinocchio.

The next morning, Geppetto told Pinocchio that a boy like him should be in school. He sent the puppet on his way, with two gold coins for lunch. But on the way, Pinocchio noticed a group of kids laughing and rollicking on a stone wall. He watched as they pushed each other and thumped their chests together.

"Are you off to school too?" Pinocchio asked.

"School's for fools," the oldest stated. "We are students of the stone wall!"

"Will I learn to be a real boy if I study with you?" Pinocchio inquired innocently.

The kids laughed. Pinocchio felt glad to have brought them such joy and joined their group at once.

Pinocchio and the kids spent the day on the stone wall. They stopped passers-by and told tales of a fox and cat prowling the woods before selling the frightened folk

"I'll call you Pinocchio!" Geppetto exclaimed.

empty bottles of "Rascal Repellent." They kicked down street signs, so travelers lost their way. When an older man asked for help with a heavy load, they called back, "What's in it for us?" Pinocchio thought this must be the nature of a real boy and he tried hard to do everything the others did. But with each deed, something odd happened.

When he tripped a baker with her arms full of loaves, the kids all laughed in approval but Pinocchio's nose wiggled a smidge. Next, he interrupted a men's ballet performance and threw half-eaten pear cores at the performers. "You can't be ballerinas, you are boys!" he shouted.

"That's right!" encouraged the others and joined in. This time, Pinocchio's nose didn't just wiggle but grew. The theater director scowled at him and evicted the rowdy lot.

At lunch, Pinocchio ordered generously from the inn to impress his new crew. When the bill came, they snuck out without paying. This time, his nose stood out from his face like a weather vane. It seemed that with each lie or bit of mischief, Pinocchio's nose grew.

"Pinocchio, you must pay for your meal. Look at what's happening!" Cinguettio landed on Pinocchio's nose. Pinocchio crossed his eyes to take in the malady.

"Oh," said Pinocchio. "But the other kids . . ."

"They have greed in their hearts where compassion should be," Cinguettio explained.

Pinocchio didn't understand. The kids were having a great time—no one was in any danger. But he left his lunch money on Cinguettio's recommendation, and his nose shrunk back.

"Hey, puppet! Shake the sawdust outta yer head," the kids called to him. "You'll miss the ride to the Land of Toys!"

Pinocchio followed their gaze to a wagon decorated with candies and a sign that read: 'Next stop—everlasting fun!' It was pulled by a team of donkeys festooned in ribbons and streamers. The wagon was packed with real kids just like Pinocchio longed to be.

"I'm not sure about this," cautioned Cinguettio.

But Pinocchio couldn't resist. He climbed aboard, dragging Cinguettio with him. They journeyed into the evening, indulging in gummies and fizzy drinks. The kids told stories about what might await them in the Land of Toys.

"I hear we each get our own bedroom in a grand mansion!" one kid said.

"I heard there are games where you win every time," chimed in another.

"Best of all, there are no grown-ups to tell you what to do, and there's NO SCHOOL!" came a cheer.

Meanwhile, Geppetto was worried when Pinocchio didn't return from school, so he set out in search of him. When he learned that Pinocchio had set off for the Land of Toys, his worry turned to fear. He set off to the beach to give chase in an old boat that bobbed at the pier. At just the moment Geppetto shoved off in his vessel, Pinocchio arrived at the Land of Toys.

It was just as described: a brilliant blaze of color and chaos. Kids could try on costumes and dance to music under a canopy of fireflies. There was a parade, carnival rides, and a fun house. There was face-painting and boat racing and an endless buffet of sweets from custards to candy floss. Everyone indulged to their heart's content.

The night finished with fireworks and the kids retired to fancy suites for bed. But as soon as the youngsters dozed, strange things started to happen. Large ears appeared on their heads. Gray tails sprouted from their trousers. Long snouts stemmed from their faces. They all turned into DONKEYS!

Pinocchio, who was not yet a real boy, was spared from becoming a real donkey. A tail tried fervently, but to no avail, to grow from Pinocchio's wooden body. But Cinguettio could see where things were headed and begged Pinocchio to flee. They raced from the place, the sound of braying and snorting reeling behind them.

Once back in town, they made straight for Geppetto's. But the door was locked, and no one was home. "Oh no!" cried Pinocchio.

"Don't worry," encouraged Cinguettio. "Just ask for help."

"But real boys don't ask for help!" Pinocchio said, making his nose grow a little.

"The heart of a real boy is powered by the help they give, and the help they receive," Cinguettio urged.

Pinocchio took a deep breath. "Excuse me neighbor!" he shouted down the street. "I need your help."

The stranger turned. It was the theater director from the ballet, who Pinocchio had offended the previous day.

"I know you!" the theater director replied. "You're the nuisance from my ballet performance. Now you want my help, eh?" he asked.

Pinocchio gulped.

"Boys can be ballerinas, you know," the theater director said sternly.

Pinocchio's heart sank. "I didn't know. I'm new at being a boy," he confessed. "It was closed-hearted of me. I'm sorry I ruined your show."

"Well, telling the truth and apologizing, those are the deeds of a heart that's growing," the theater director observed with a smile. "I can see you are a work in progress. Your papa went looking for you out at sea. Follow me."

The theater director led the way to the beach. Pinocchio scrambled up a rock and looked out to the horizon. There was no sign of a boat, but without hesitation Pinocchio dove into the waves. He swam and swam as fast as his wooden legs could kick. Suddenly, he felt a surge of movement beneath him and a great fish rose up out of the water. It was a mile-long and as tall as a castle. Its mouth was wide open and Pinocchio was washed right into the beast.

Down Pinocchio slid, deep into the vast cavern which was the belly of the fish.

"Helloooo," he called, into the darkness.

"Helloooo, helloooo," it echoed back.

Then one extra, "Hello?" was heard.

"Is someone there?" Pinocchio asked into the void.

"Just an old man looking for his son," a voice came back.

"What a coincidence, I'm just a boy looking for his papa," Pinocchio replied.

Footsteps sounded and out of the haze Pinocchio spied a lantern. Holding it was a water-logged Geppetto!

"Papa!" Pinocchio exclaimed.

"Pinocchio?" Geppetto ran to hug his boy. "I have an idea of how we can get out of here."

Geppetto led Pinocchio to the fish's mouth where a small boat lay waiting. The two climbed aboard.

"We need to get the fish to sneeze and shoot us out of its mouth." Geppetto said. "But I'm not sure how..."

"I know!" Pinocchio exclaimed. He began to talk. "A real boy is someone who never asks for help and never says he's sorry!"

His nose grew.

"Who's never happy with what he has, and always wants more!'

Again, his nose doubled.

"Who doesn't care about other people, and cares only for himself!"

By now, Pinocchio's nose nearly reached the roof of the fish's mouth.

"I have the heart of a real boy!" he shouted. His nose grew until it collided with the body of the fish. And then, unexpectedly it zapped back to its original size. Before father and son knew what was happening, the great beast let out a large sneeze.

"Ahhhhh . . . CHOOOOOOOO!"

The blast sent Pinocchio and Geppetto through the mouth of the fish and out into the sea. They rode the little boat to shore, where the Blue Fairy and Cinguettio were waiting.

"I know what the heart of a real boy is," Pinocchio panted as he climbed out.

"What is it?" asked the Blue Fairy with a knowing smile.

"A heart that is open and understanding," he beamed, "that gives and receives and loves bravely."

Geppetto had tears in his eyes. Cinguettio gave Pinocchio's finger a squeeze.

"Wow," smiled the Blue Fairy. "You've done it. Put your hand to your chest."

Pinocchio did as he was told and felt a subtle thumping beneath his palm. With each thump his body become more and more like a boy's. His hair grew soft, his skin supple, and his eyes moist. A warm glow grew around him and spread around Geppetto too.

From that day forward, the glow stayed with the pair. Pinocchio and Geppetto worked side by side in the woodshop doing repairs for the town. Later, they turned the woodshop into a crafts club called Heartsmiths. There, Pinocchio taught students of all ages how to turn a single block of wood into a fish-shaped bowl, and began a tradition of filling each bowl with notes from the heart.

Rumpelstiltskin

Once upon a time, hidden in a wood lay a small homestead. The people who lived there had magical powers and had fled their faraway homeland to protect these gifts. But it wasn't easy being outsiders. People were wary of them, so they found it difficult to find work.

Among their hardship shone one bright spot, a promising young man. The homestead pooled their meager resources and put forth an application for him to attend the King's Crown Preparatory School. They hoped that if he could get a great education, he could lift up his people.

Beside the wood, ran a delicate stream with a mill. The mill was home to a miller and his daughter Philomena. The miller saw great potential in his daughter and put in an application for her too to attend King's Crown. It was competitive to get into and the miller embellished her application with the promise that Philomena could "spin straw into gold."

King's Crown accepted the young man and Philomena immediately, and sent for them in a lavish carriage.

"You can call me Slink," the young man said eagerly.

"Is that your real name?" Philomena asked.

"It's more of a nickname," the boy replied. For his real name was jumble of letters and a pile of sounds. He didn't dare arrive at a new school with a moniker like that, it would reveal his status as a homesteader.

"In that case, I'm Mena," Philomena said.

As the carriage pulled up to the school the two could see it was an intimidating place. Tall bell towers loomed on either side of a broad entrance. Students scuttled from place to place with purpose. The principal's office was their first destination.

"I'll put you straight into Advanced Textiles, given your talents for spinning straw into gold," he announced to Philomena. "As for you Ru—"

"It's Slink sir," the boy interrupted quickly.

"Right, Slink, I'll have you start in the Foundations class," he said with a smile.

The two new students walked to their classrooms together. When Philomena entered the textiles room a look of panic crossed her face. Slink thought he knew why. Inside sat the school's cool crew. The air was filled with their laughter, inside jokes, and jests. They played the ever so cool "Gems and Giants" game with buttons and rhinestones. Slink knew instantly he wanted to be one of them. Philomena, on the other hand, had noticed a pile of straw at her work station. She turned to leave.

Slink reached out and stopped her.

"Where are you going? These are the coolest kids in school. I'd give anything to be one of them!" he said, eyes wide.

"Are you kidding?" Philomena whispered anxiously. "I can't go in there. My father lied on my application, and everyone thinks I can spin straw into gold! I can't do that, can you?!"

"As matter of fact, I can," Slink confessed.

Philomena perked up. "Really?! Will you do it for me? If you do, I'll get you in with the cool crowd!"

Slink pondered the opportunity. As a new student he needed to fit in, and as an outsider he needed to succeed. "OK, I'll sneak in and do your work for you in the night. Just put in a good word for me, yeah?"

Philomena nodded in agreement. "I owe you!" she whispered as she passed into the room. The crowd swarmed around her, eager to meet the sensational new student who could spin straw into gold.

"Welcome!" they beamed. "Can't wait to see your talents in action."

Slink watched through the door. He caught Philomena's eye.

"Hey, who's that peeping in on us?" someone said.

"That's nobody," Philomena said, lowering her eyes.

That evening, true to his name and his promise, Slink slunk into the textiles room. As he worked, he sang a little song:

"Round about, round about,
My praise Mena foretold!
 Twist away, twist away,
 Turn straw into gold!"

Before long the straw was a pile of gold ribbon. When the class came in the next day, everyone was in awe.

"Mena, you are so talented! You simply must do this for our Winter Ball," her peers crooned.

"Our crew always does the planning, you have to be on the committee," they begged.

Even the principal popped in to admire the work.

"Yes, Mena, you should be on the committee for the Winter Ball," he insisted. "All our trustees will be there to see our best and brightest shine."

Mena gulped and excused herself to find Slink. He was in an out-of-the-way spot on campus. "Oh, hey, Mena!" he said, perking up. "Did you tell the crew about me? Maybe I could sit at their table at the Winter Ball?"

"What?! You haven't really come up yet," Mena said, bending the truth. "But speaking of the Winter Ball, I need your help again."

"Oh, they liked my work!" Slink lit up. "I'll help you, but promise me this time you'll talk me up."

"I promise," Mena said.

Mena arranged for the principal to provide enough straw to deck the halls for the ball. That night she piled the straw high on her work station and headed to bed. Slink snuck in again and sung quietly to himself as he worked his magic.

"Round about, round about,

My cool factor they'll behold!

Reel away, reel away,

Turn straw into gold!"

In the morning, a resounding celebration of the gold was heard throughout the school.

"Can you believe it!?" the students and teachers exclaimed. "Such artistry! We are so lucky to have a student like Mena."

But it wasn't her glow to bask in, it was Slink's and he was getting impatient. He cornered Mena by the door to her class, but just then, the cool crew sidled up and Slink was pushed to the side.

"You won't believe what the principal has in store!" the students said excitedly to Mena. "He is planning a live performance of your straw-to-gold spinning at the Ball! Once everyone sees your talent, you'll be the toast of the after party!"

Mena went pale. Slink went wide eyed. As the cool crew wound off, Slink turned to Mena. "You're really in a jam this time," he observed.

"You think?!" Mena looked at Slink pleadingly.

Slink shook his head. "After party . . . that sounds amazing. I'll help you one last time, but you have to get me into that party," he said.

"You'll be on the guest list, I promise." Mena assured him. On her way to bed, she popped by the headteacher's office to secure his spot.

The night of the Ball arrived. Gold ribbon draped every surface. From chairs to bleachers, columns to mirrors. Everything was adorned in Slink's handiwork and Mena's lie. Mena regarded the room with fear, but Slink admired it with pride. He'd done a good thing, he thought. Surely, he would be rewarded with entry into the cool crew.

When the stage was lit for Mena's performance, Slink crept beneath the stage. They had arranged for Mena to pass straw through a missing floorboard to Slink, who would then send gold ribbon back up. It was hot and cramped while Slink performed the task. Above, the illusion weighed on Mena too. Her fingers shook and she was drenched in sweat.

When it was over, Mena expected to feel buoyant with relief, but instead she felt ill. She wanted to go straight to bed, but Slink raced to her side.

"You promised me," he reminded Mena.

So, off they went to the after party. It was held at the king's palace and the "who's who" of the kingdom were in attendance. Candlelit chandeliers soared over buffets and drinks bars. Fountains flowed into pools and the whole thing was bordered with cozy seating where the cool crew perched. All that stood between Slink and his place among them was the velvet security rope.

"Name, please!" barked a guard.

"Slink," Slink said hopefully.

"And Mena, Philomena," Mena added.

"Ah right, this way m'lady. Sorry young man, I don't see you on the list." The guard held a hand up.

Slink stood, mouth agape. He glared at Mena. "You didn't put my name on the list? After what I did for you?!"

"I did!" Mena cried.

"I can give you three tries to offer a name listed here," said the guard. "After that, we have to eject you."

Slink wondered why his name wasn't on the list. Then he realized with alarm. It was his given name that was on the list! The name that would give away his origins as a homesteader. The one that would make him different.

Slink confronted Mena in front of the growing line of party-goers.

"You need to get me on that list!" he said.

Mena held firm. "I told you, I did. I asked the headteacher directly."

"I mean you need to get me as Slink on that list," he explained.

"But why?" Mena asked.

"My real name is . . . embarrassing. It shows I'm a homesteader," Slink confesssed.

Heads turned at his words. The cool crew moved from their perch to the entry.

"See?" Slink said, gesturing at the crowd. "I don't want to draw attention to that part of me."

"Why not? It's what made you want to help me, even when I let you down," Mena said. "You don't need to be afraid to be yourself."

The assembled crowd nodded encouragingly. Slink took a deep breath. Maybe Mena was right. "It starts with an R," he started. The guard scanned the list.

"RAMONE, RICHMOND, RAFAEL, RORY, RASHEED, RUFUS. . ."

"No, it's. . . Rumpelstiltskin!" Slink said, his eyes closed against the jeers he feared.

"Here it is!" said the guard with a smile. "What a distinctive name!"

"It means 'gold turner' in my native language," Slink explained.

"What are you saying?" asked a member of the cool crew.

"He's saying he's the one who can turn straw into gold, not me," Mena confessed, looking at the floor.

"I'm saying, I'm not hiding my true self anymore," Slink said with new-found confidence. "And neither should you," he said, turning to Mena. "You don't need magic to be accepted. You just need to be yourself."

Mena and Slink strode into the party. For the first time, they had nothing to hide.

King's Crown school was changed forever. Students mixed freely and were encouraged to bring their unique histories into the classroom. The velvet ropes were cast aside, and all were welcome at the Winter Ball After Party.

After Slink and Mina graduated, they returned home to share what they had learnt with their hometowns. From time to time, Slink stopped by the mill to teach Mena and her father how to spin straw into gold, with this cheery song and a hint of magic:

> "Round about, round about,
> Let everyone behold!
> Reel away, reel away,
> Don't hide your inner gold!"

From time to time, Slink stopped by the mill to teach Mena and her father how to spin straw into gold.

Jack and the Beanstalk

Once upon a time, in a quiet row of thatched cottages, there lived a boy named Jack, his two moms, and their cow named Sweet Cream. His parents worked in a nearby town and Jack spent his days tending the garden. Though Jack had a green thumb, it was a lot to take care of and he was often lonely.

Each morning his parents joined the parade of residents from the lane as they strode off to work. Jack watched them from the window with curiosity. They were all smartly dressed. Many carried leather satchels and gold watches on their way to the market, and the profitable profession of trading. In the evenings, they'd stream back to the cottages with baskets steaming with warm food and arms filled with new goods to improve their homes and gardens.

"These are people who can look after their families," Jack thought aloud to his cow. "This is who I shall become."

So, one day when he was old enough, Jack struck out with the commuters to try his hand at the market. He brought his family's only asset, their cow Sweet Cream.

At the market it wasn't easy. Jack felt discouraged. Everyone was trading fancy items, and they already had relationships formed. No one wanted Sweet Cream, and Jack didn't see how he'd ever be like the other traders. But just as he was about to leave, a stranger approached him.

"Interested in trading that cow?" the stranger proposed.

It was Jack's first opportunity and he didn't want to miss it. "She's been in the family a long while, what are you offering?" he said.

"I will give you five magic beans!" the stranger offered.

Magic beans, Jack thought. Perhaps this was how things worked. So he nodded, took the magic beans and gave the stranger the cow.

When he reached home, Jack's moms were less than impressed.

"You traded away our cow for some beans?" his mom sighed, while his mama added the beans to the garden seed mix in a planter.

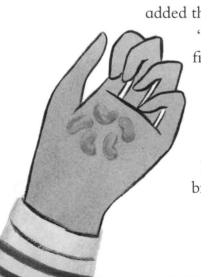

"Don't worry, they're magic!" Jack said hopefully. "They are my first small steps toward a future of new comforts for us."

When Jack woke the next day, he saw that a great beanstalk had grown from the magic beans! Jack rushed to climb it. Now he was sure he had made a good trade.

At the top of the beanstalk Jack's hopes were confirmed. Before him lay a towering city where everything was bigger. Bigger plants, bigger roads, bigger homes, bigger buildings. There were even much bigger people. They had legs like tree trunks and feet like boats. It appeared he had climbed right into a giant's realm.

"Aaah!" gasped Jack. He had heard giants were dangerous and grisly and would grind your bones to make their bread. So he rushed to get out of there. He was just about to scramble down the beanstalk when something caught his eye.

It was a market stall with a great goose, and the bird had just laid a golden egg. Beside that stood another marvelous stall, packed with instruments including a harp that was singing. Jack saw more stalls with giant foods and garments so big that one sock could cover his whole chimney. At the end of the row of stalls, overflowing bags of coins rested on the ground.

An idea struck Jack. With just one gold egg he could rise instantly to the top. That thing would trade brilliantly, he thought to himself. Everyone would want it. Then, as if Jack had willed it to happen, a golden egg rolled away from the stall toward him. He caught the egg with a hug. But at just that moment a few giants drew close.

"Fe, Fi, Fo, Fum," they sang.

Jack scrambled down the beanstalk, golden egg in arms. He raced into the cottage, where his folks were beginning their day.

"You won't believe it. Those magic beans sprouted a beanstalk that is my shortcut to success!" Jack called out, gesturing up the beanstalk. "You can both retire! I can provide us with everything we need and then some. Aren't you pleased?"

"Jack, what are you thinking? There are no short cuts to success," his mama said. "If you want to work your way up the trader's track you've got to start at the bottom."

"But atop the beanstalk is an abundance of amazing things," Jack persisted, presenting the egg.

"You can't take things that don't belong to you!" his mom asserted, and cast the egg aside.

Jack didn't understand. He thought he'd be the provider all his neighbors were.

"I ought to chop that beanstalk down right now." Jack's mom reached for an axe.

"No, no!" Jack cried and scrambled up the beanstalk to deter her.

On his return up the beanstalk Jack considered his parents' words. Maybe he hadn't illustrated his point well enough.

He decided this time he'd bring down something of higher value. What said success better than a singing harp? But this would be a riskier prospect, he'd have to really watch out for the giants.

Jack made his way to the trading table and surveyed the scene. He wrapped his arms around the harp and slowly slid it toward the beanstalk.

"I smell trouble!" boomed a voice. (Even though they are so far away from things, giants have an excellent sense of smell).

"Nah, that just Fugue's farts. Excuse yourself, Fugue!" another voice replied.

"I thought I smelled the human world. . . " the voice trailed off.

Jack hastened down the beanstalk like he was on a slide. The harp was awakened and it sang out.

"La la la la laaaaaaaaaa."

It was time for the morning commute. Jack's neighbors noticed the glittering harp and heard the bright voice and took a detour to his garden.

"Wow, Jack, what market are you playing at?" someone asked.

"Looks like your folks will be set for life," another one commented, glancing up at the beanstalk with raised eyebrows.

Jack stared up at the beanstalk too. With one more acquisition his neighbor would be right, Jack and his family could be set for life. He could provide everything their hearts desired. So that afternoon, while the neighborhood was at work, Jack ventured once more up the beanstalk.

This time Jack popped up right in the middle of the giant's marketplace. Terrified, he ducked beneath a table and closed his eyes tight to shut out the horror he anticipated. He imagined rolling heads and drooling monsters. Instead this is what he heard:

"Grace! Come check out the eggs, there's one missing!" said a deep voice.

"Oh T-Bone, I knew it was a bad investment," a gentle voice lamented.

"Huh?" thought Jack.

"There's that smell again," a familiar third voice broke into Jack's thoughts.

"Yes, I smell it too," said the giant called Grace.

"I think it's coming from under the table," said the giant called T-Bone.

The two giants peered under the table and discovered Jack.

"Just where did you come from?" asked T-Bone with a face as stern as a stone wall.

"I'm Jack! I live in the world below the beanstalk. Please don't eat me!" Jack pleaded hastily.

"Eat you? Why would we eat you? We are fruitarians!" Grace pulled Jack out from under the table.

"What are you doing up here anyway?" T-Bone pondered.

"Uh, nothing." Jack held his hands up in surrender.

The two giants peered under the table and discovered Jack.

"What's that on your hands?" asked Grace, coming in for a closer look.

"Looks like bits of gold," observed T-Bone.

Sure enough, gold dust covered Jack's hands and dappled his pants. Jack gulped.

"Well?" the giants asked expectantly.

"I think a gold harp and a golden egg found its way down the beanstalk," Jack sort-of confessed.

"A harp and an egg?" repeated Grace. "Oh no, this means we won't be able to pay our sales team and they have others, wee ones, old ones, who depend on them."

Jack's error began to sink in. He had stolen to get ahead. But in doing so, he had put someone else behind.

"Gotta run!" Jack said and he raced for the beanstalk, trembling as he descended. He nearly made it all the way home when he saw a terrible sight. In his very own garden were the golden egg and coins. A crowd of onlookers had assembled, and some were climbing the beanstalk.

"Stop!" Jack cried out. "Don't touch those things! Get the axe!"

Suddenly the beanstalk swayed. Jack looked up and saw the faces of the giants peering down at him from above.

"Is that our egg down there?" wondered Grace.

"Is that our harp?" questioned T-Bone.

"It's not what you think," Jack pleaded. "Well . . . it is what you think, but I'll give them back."

"Why ever did you take them?" T-Bone asked.

"It looked like an opportunity to get ahead quickly. To take care of my parents," Jack admitted.

"I know that pressure," T-Bone reflected. "I have a lot of people looking to me to keep them well cared for, when really I'd rather just play that harp!"

"Really?" said Grace, looking surprised. "We can make that happen, T. You shouldn't feel like you have to carry a heavier load than anyone else. No one should."

"I can chop down the stalk and you'll never have to see us again," Jack offered. Jack's neighbors and family waited with bated breath.

"No, wait, what is growing in your garden there?" T-Bone inquired.

"Just fruits and veggies," Jack said honestly.

"They look fantastic," T-Bone commented. "How'd you like to try an honest trade. You keep the items you took, and we get fresh produce from the garden. It'd be a real treasure to us."

The assembled party in Jack's garden all nodded. His parents put down the axes and both nodded and so Jack nodded too.

"Congratulations!" everyone cheered.

"Looks like you can be both a fine trader and a fine gardener," Jack's mom observed.

"But in this family, we provide for one another, not just one person for all the others," his mama added.

Grace interrupted the merriment. "Looks like we have a deal. Come on up and let's shake on it." And with that Grace and T-Bone reached down from the clouds. Jack climbed up to meet them and gave their giant hands a gentle squeeze.

The beanstalk stayed up as a monument to the new trade relations between Jack and the giants. Jack returned his focus to his true passion as a gardener. His favorite days were market days, when he'd hoist a fresh harvest up to the giants' realm. T-Bone would play the harp beautifully, and Jack could see that delivering on one's own dream was the best thing you could provide to those you loved.

Quasimodo

Once upon a time, a grand temple stood at the heart of a sunny city. The temple was an architectural marvel made up of two towers resting on a great stone platform, which in turn rested on many flights of stairs, so that the whole thing could overlook a beautiful lake and town center. It was embellished with animated carvings of amazing creatures. The temple functioned as a community center, a place of learning and—most importantly—a sanctuary where people could go when they needed help.

So, when one day a baby appeared on the steps of the temple, the priest Frollo gladly took it in. He named the baby Quasimodo and brought the youngster up within the temple. As Quasimodo grew, it was clear that he was different. He became a great tall kid with bright eyes. Yet his body was hunched and bunched, and his legs were not quite matched. When Quasimodo was a young man, it became clear that this was how he would be forever.

Quasimodo didn't like going out for fear of how people would react to his different body. So Frollo found a role for him as bell ringer which kept him out of the public eye. Each day, Quasimodo cleaned the bells and rang them to mark significant hours.

It was a simple life, and sometimes it left Quasimodo lonely. He'd cry in the belfry when he was feeling especially low. He'd talk to the carved faces on the exterior of the tower: a lion, an eagle, and a funny-looking monster. He'd even do voices for them. "Oh, hello Bellows, meet Wingding. What's that? You are tired of looking west? Bellows, tell us what you see to the east." Above all, Quasimodo longed to have friends that were real.

One of the hardest and loneliest days for Quasimodo was FoolsFest. This was an annual gathering of colorful entertainers and smart speakers. It drew a crowd of merriment to the town center that Quasimodo could glimpse from his belfry. He'd observe the fun with great interest but didn't dare join in for fear of drawing attention to himself, or getting in the way.

One particular year, the town found itself on the verge of great change. A new civilization was growing nearby. Quasimodo's town was small and many of the tradespeople had moved away, so it was thought to be unimportant by the new civilization. They planned to take it over, and this was to be the last FoolsFest.

A new speaker called Esmerelda took the stage. She told of the new civilization, how they had come to her hometown too.

"They tear down old buildings to make way for new," Esmerelda warned the rapt crowd. "They'll do away with the plaza and fill in the lake."

Quasimodo was troubled. He loved the town. The buildings that surrounded him were, at times, his only friends. Where would people go who were in need? Where would *he* go? He couldn't let the place get torn down.

After the speech was finished, Quasimodo agonized about what to do. He searched for Frollo to seek his help, but was disappointed when Frollo told him, "There is nothing I can do, son. People have been leaving this town for years. Sometimes you just have to make way for history."

At first Quasimodo accepted Frollo's stance. After all, he rarely even went out in public, so what could he do? Quasimodo retreated to his belfry. He looked out over the town square. But as he watched the townspeople enjoying a silly mask contest, he wondered if it was right to let this all disappear. Could there be other people who felt the same? He decided to get a little closer to the action to find out.

After dark, Quasimodo covered himself in a cape and snuck out! He crawled over his carved friends who guarded the belfry, down the side of the tower, and down the many stairs to the square. Everyone at the festival was awaiting the crowning of the King of Fools. Quasimodo spotted Esmeralda chatting with the townspeople and moved closer.

"We can't let this happen," one said.

"What can we do?" another asked.

"I'll tell you what can be done," Esmeralda said. "If we get enough different people to support preserving the town center and the temple we can negotiate."

"Well there are plenty of us, but we need some powerful voices to join in," a townsperson reflected. "That's the only way we'll be heard."

Surprising himself, Quasimodo's soft voice broke in. "Maybe someone from the temple?"

"Who said that?" Esmerelda asked. Everyone turned to look at the cloaked figure.

"A leader from the temple could help. That's what they do—help," Quasimodo explained.

"That's exactly right!" Esmerelda said. "Do you know someone there?"

"I live there," Quasimodo admitted.

"Are you a priest?" Esmerelda asked.

Quasimodo was nervous. Esmeralda was so outgoing, so clear in her convictions. And he felt so self-conscious. "Not exactly. . ." he admitted.

"No matter! It's a brilliant idea. You're our king of the festival!" Esmerelda cheered. Without hesitation, she grabbed Quasimodo's hand and raced him to the pedestal where a crown awaited. The comedian introduced him as "King of FoolsFest" and a shower of candy was thrown from the crowd! Before Quasimodo knew it, his hood was flung off, and the crown placed upon his head.

The crowd gasped. "It's the belfry boy!" someone cried.

Quasimodo was terrified. He had never been the center of a conversation, much less a crowd, and he fell to the ground. Seeing his distress, the crowd quietly dispersed.

"I should have stayed in the belfry," Quasimodo gulped, seeing the townsfolk leave.

"No, no!" Esmeralda said, kneeling beside him. "They only left because they saw you were uncomfortable. They threw sweets to celebrate you, not to mock you!"

But Quasimodo didn't believe her. He slunk back to the temple, where Frollo was waiting.

"Quasi, what happened?" Frollo asked. "What were you thinking, going out there? Are you OK?"

"It was scary," Quasimodo admitted, wiping a tear from

his face. "But I learned something. If you and the others in the temple joined in standing up for our town, we could save it!"

Frollo shook his head. "Oh, Quasi, you are new to the great wide world. I really don't see a way to save our place," he said. "The new civilization is just too big and too powerful."

"But—"

"I'd like you to stay in the belfry," Frollo instructed. "If there is going to be an uprising, it'll be dangerous to be outside."

Quasimodo, feeling powerless, consented to being locked in the belfry. He paced his room. He could feel the tension mounting outside. A notice was pasted in the square which showed the plans for the changes to come. Just as Esmerelda had foretold, it described filling in the lake and taking down the temple. It even announced a start date: that evening! Quasimodo could hear the townspeople talking anxiously.

"What if we need fresh water?"

"Where will we keep all our community supplies like tools, wagons, and books?"

"If a visitor comes in need of help where can they go?"

That was the last straw for Quasimodo. Even though he was uncomfortable in public, he was willing to work on it if it meant preserving his temple as a safe haven for others. He had to make his voice heard, but knew he'd never convince Frollo. He'd have to sneak out again. He reached for his cloak but stopped, thinking of what Esmerelda had said. Maybe people weren't scared of him, after all. "No one even mentioned my shape," he reminded himself aloud. Then Esmerelda's voice rung in his head.

"If we get enough different people to support us, we can negotiate!" she'd said.

So with a deep breath, Quasimodo slid down the side of the tower.

As he ran to find Esmerelda, a great rumble could be heard nearby. It was the sound of the demolition crew advancing. The clamor propeled Quasimodo through alleys and corners. He found a staircase and heard another huge rumble. This time, it was the sound of lots of people talking. Cautiously, he went down the steps.

Quasimodo soon entered an immense hall hidden beneath the streets. All the townspeople who had gathered there turned to look at him. Quasimodo felt scared, but he knew he had to speak.

"The tear down crew is nearly here!" he said softly.

"Speak up!" a voice called from the back. It was Esmerelda's and it lifted him.

"If we unite, we can show the newcomers what this town means to us," he said, more loudly this time. "Together we have enough people to block the demolition. But we have to hurry. It's nearly sunset!"

Esmerelda pushed past the crowd and up the stairs, then led the march to the town square. The townspeople assembled in front of the temple. The demolition crew had arrived with wrecking balls and catapults to change the town forever.

*As each person spoke, they linked arms and formed
a chain across the square.*

"We, the people of this town, ask you to reconsider the tear down of our beloved square and safe haven." Quasimodo extended a hand of negotiation to the foreperson leading the demolition.

"You dare try and stop this project?" the foreperson shouted over the noise.

"Our new civilization has unprecedented power, what contribution could this small town offer?" another worker added.

"Yeah, what have you got worth saving?" the foreperson said.

Quasimodo stepped forward. "Me," he said.

The foreperson looked taken aback.

"And me," said Esmerelda.

"And me," a familiar voice added. It was Frollo! Quasimodo looked at him in shock. Frollo was smiling and he had the rest of the temple leaders along with him. "And me," each of them said.

"And me, and me, and me, and me."

A trail of voices rang out from the townspeople. As each person spoke, they linked arms and formed a chain across the square.

"Well, if so many feel so strongly," the foreperson said, "we'll open negotiations." They sighed and packed up their wagons.

"What swayed your mind?" Quasimodo asked Frollo, when they had gone.

"I realized; the temple has been your sanctuary—not because it provided protection, but because it is where you grew into someone wonderful." Frollo put an arm around Quasimodo. "Real sanctuary is not bars, it's an open door."

In the next few months, Esmeralda, Frollo, and Quasimodo brought back tradespeople to restore the town and temple to its original glory. Quasimodo proposed that the temple be a shared venue for the townspeople and the new civilization. A spot to assemble art and books, where everyone could attend concerts and festivals. Most importantly it would be a welcoming centre for newcomers, complete with accommodations for those in need. The new civilization agreed and built a grand extension with seating and stages to suit the masses.

The town and its people flourished. Quasimodo was once again crowned king of the annual festival, although this time it was called: FriendFest.

To those who protect landmarks great and small, so they remain sanctuaries for us all

KING OF FRIENDFEST

The Snow Man

In the land of the midnight sun, where summer light lasts through the night and winter is a parade of darkness, there once sat a small cottage. It was home to a family who filled the place with love and affection. They enjoyed cozy suppers round a wood burning stove, busy breakfast over its top, and afternoons of drawing and telling stories while toasting their toes near it.

One day, a big snowfall laid a soft white blanket over everything the eye could see. It beckoned the family outside. They grabbed their snowshoes and donned their warmest woollens. The father wore goggles and the mother rubbed the little ones' faces with oil to protect against the cold.

Out they bounded into the snow. It flew up around them like star dust. As the day wore on, the snow grew wet and clingy. It was perfect for building.

"Let's build something!" the father suggested.

"Yes! Yes!" the children cheered.

They gathered snow from all around the yard, rolled it into big rounds and stacked them in a tower.

"It's as tall as you, Mom," the youngest child observed.

"It can be a snow man," said the eldest child, placing their hat upon the top of the tower.

"Here is his bowtie," said the father, pulling out two pieces of broken tile.

"It needs some eyes," added the youngest child, who pressed acorns into the snowy surface. Beneath the eyes the mother laid a string of berries to form a smile.

Their family dog ran out from the house, a carrot in its jaws. They lodged it in the Snow Man's face as a cheerful nose. The days were short in winter and as the sun sank, the family retired to the warmth of their home.

Only the dog remained outside and inspected the new yard resident. She sniffed and circled and settled on a spot to squat, when all of a sudden a voice cried out.

"Ah! What's this? Are you going to paint me yellow?!"

The dog laughed. "I was going to relieve myself before I snuggle in the house with the family." She nodded toward the house. "They don't like it when I do it in there."

"Can I come in with you?" asked the innocent Snow Man.

"Have you slush for brains?" barked the dog. "That is a roasty, toasty home. You can't possibly go in there. You'll become a puddle!"

The Snow Man looked sad.

"Cheer up!" said the dog. "You've plenty of creatures to hang with out here. Pleasant folk stroll this route often. They'll surely stop and visit you." And off the dog went, to curl up with the family by the fire.

The Snow Man watched mournfully through the window. He saw the father wrap the little ones in a blanket and nuzzle them with his scratchy beard as they wriggled and giggled. The mother playfully threw pillows and the Snow Man longed to share in the light-heartedness. When the family gathered to enjoy cocoa, the father tossed marshmallows and the mother caught them in her drink with a wink. The Snow Man wished he had someone to eat marshmallows with.

The next day, just as the dog predicted, many people passed by. They were all in tidy pairs. Two old friends shared a laugh over a scroll of red paper. A twosome came arm in arm, one listening intently to the other, each holding a pink envelope. A young man and woman burrowed in a carriage, resting their heads together under a blanket decorated with hearts.

"It's Valentine's Day," remarked the dog, seeing that the Snow Man was curious.

"What's that?" the Snow Man asked eagerly.

"It's an ancient festival celebrating the sweetness of love," explained the dog.

"I saw people exchange paper tokens shaped like hearts," observed the Snow Man. "I should like to do that."

"Well, you'll need a sweetheart," said the dog.

"Sweetheart?" asked the Snow Man. "What's that?"

"Someone whom you are drawn to and long to embrace," explained the dog.

"Oh, I know exactly who my sweetheart is!" said the Snow Man excitedly.

The dog was surprised. "You do?"

"Oh, I long to sit beside that wonderful Snow Man there in the neighboring yard. He is sensational. He has a blissful grin and top hat, I just can't stop admiring him."

"I dunno, a Snow Man paired with another Snow Man?" said the dog, sniffing. "Why don't we find you a more suitable valentine? A lady, made of the same winter

whimsy as you? I've just the match!" The dog bounded away, leaving the Snow Man alone with his thoughts.

Later, the dog returned with a small gnome. She had a fluffy plume of white hair and a tall red hat.

"Who are you?" asked the Snow Man.

"I go by many names: Haltijia, Nisse, Tomte, but you can call me Karly," the little lady said.

The Snow Man was keen to be as happy as all the couples he'd seen, so he made an effort to get to know Karly. But while Karly was friendly, the Snow Man felt no warm glow. He didn't long to sit beside her or yearn to lay his head on her shoulder. In fact, Karly's shoulder was too far away to reach. The dog could tell the two weren't exactly well-matched and scampered off to find a new valentine. The Snow Man bid Karly farewell.

The dog returned with a creature much taller.

"This is Iku Turso," the dog said, "a water queen."

Iku Turso was shaped like a great bell with long tentacles. She slid toward the Snow Man, looking uncomfortable.

"What's the matter?" the Snow Man worried.

"I'm not used to being out of the water," Iku Turso explained.

"I'm made of water if it helps?" offered the Snow Man with a chuckle. "We have that in common, and we are a comparable size. Could you be my valentine?"

"Oh," Iku Turso squirmed. "I'm sorry, I actually have my heart set on another."

"Oh. May I ask what makes you certain of them?" the Snow Man asked, disappointed.

"I am the most myself around them," Iku Turso said, blushing.

"Oh, I see. So I should be myself with my valentine?" the Snow Man asked.

"Yeah!" brightened Iku Turso. "Don't worry. You're a great frozen fellow, you'll meet a better match." And she slid back toward the sea.

The dog sniffed and circled. "I've got it!" she said, and set off once again.

Soon a great crunching of snow was heard and from a line of trees a fantastic creature appeared.

"Allow me to present Miss Otso!" beamed the dog. "She is one of the most revered northern magical creatures." She bowed and made way for a bear with a crown of trees upon her head.

"I'm Otso. It's nice to meet you," spoke the bear with a regal voice.

The Snow Man was impressed. They were nearly the same shape and Otso brought warmth and friendliness with her. Yet the Snow Man, in spite of their compatibility and easy rapport, didn't feel for Otso what he felt for the Snow Man next door.

Otso could tell. "I sense you have someone else on your mind. Why don't you tell me about them?" she said.

"Well, if I'm honest, and I know it sounds different," the Snow Man slowly opened up, "I can't stop thinking about the Snow Man just over the fence."

"I see." Otso raised her brows.

"When I look in the house, and see how happy the people make one another, I wonder, who makes the other Snow Man happy? Could I be that someone?"

"Hmmm," Otso pondered.

"I know it's not what the dog has in mind for me but. . ."

"But you're drawn to the Snow Man." Otso finished the Snow Man's thought knowingly.

The two sat silently.

"Well, perhaps the first thing would be to see how the Snow Man feels about you," Otso suggested.

"But what if he rejects me?"

"Well there's only one way to find out," offered the dog, nudging some craft paper and ink toward the Snow Man.

With encouragement, the Snow Man drafted a sweet valentine. It was a big red heart with a simple note: *I've admired you from over the fence, and now I wish to come near. Would you like to be my valentine? And get to know my cheer?*

The dog delivered the valentine to the Snow Man next door. The neighbor Snow Man read the card and beamed. He looked across the fence for his admirer, then drew a coal from his buttoned belly and scrawled a response. The dog ran out with the card once again.

The two made an excellent pair indeed.

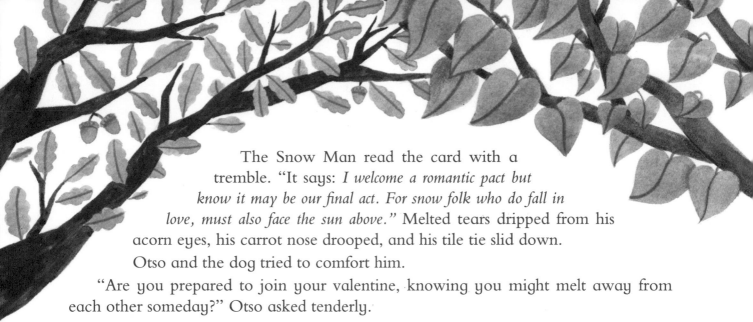

The Snow Man read the card with a tremble. "It says: *I welcome a romantic pact but know it may be our final act. For snow folk who do fall in love, must also face the sun above.*" Melted tears dripped from his acorn eyes, his carrot nose drooped, and his tile tie slid down.

Otso and the dog tried to comfort him.

"Are you prepared to join your valentine, knowing you might melt away from each other someday?" Otso asked tenderly.

The Snow Man found his smile.

And so it was, the Snow Man slid to meet his neighbor. He soon learned the chap was called Lumi. The two made an excellent pair indeed. They had so much in common: like-minded families who built them and a shared interest in the night sky. They made the most of the quiet evenings and shared their wish to be together long after winter passed them by.

The days grew longer and warmer, and the Snow Man and his valentine began to melt. As the Snow Man's waist and face shrunk, his core was laid bare and something was revealed! At first, all that could be seen was an acorn. But as more snow melted, more of the Snow Man's center was discovered. Until finally, on a warm spring day, in the place where the Snow Man had stood, gleamed an oak sapling. And where his valentine Lumi once stood, there was a sturdy shoot of a catalpa tree.

As the families returned to the yard for spring planting, they couldn't help but notice the stunning new additions.

"Why look at this . . . have you ever seen something so lovely?" exclaimed the father.

"It must have been wrapped up in all that deep snow. In our Snow Man I suppose," the mother replied.

"Look, another new tree beside it. What are the chances?" wondered the eldest child.

During the days and years that followed, the two trees grew steadily. One shaded the other, they passed nutrients in the soil below between them, and they offered homes to animals like birds and squirrels. The family too grew around them. And the ageing dog often curled up in their shade. On lovely summer days, the light from the sun hugged the heart-shaped leaves of the catalpa tree, and showered the yard below in their silhouettes, bringing a hint of Valentine's Day to the longest days of the year.

Prince Charming

In a familiar land, many spins of the sun ago, lived Prince Charming. His father the king raised him to be a model citizen and an ambassador of the throne. He was expected to act with grace, as he represented the monarchy. This meant no eccentricities, no hobbies, and certainly no going "off script."

From an early age Charming was in the spotlight. He posed for portraits, featured in parades, was sketched onto greeting cards . . . His face even embossed coins and candy wrappers. Every appearance was carefully curated by his father, the king.

"Move the playing cards from view," the king requested at a portrait sitting.

"But that's my Knight of the Golden Shield game, I just got good at it," Charming lamented.

"Tidy up the boy's hair, and is that nail paint? Take it off," the king instructed the royal barber prior to a parade.

"But all the kids are wearing it!" Charming pleaded. But his voice went unheard.

One day, while riding his pegasus Laser, Charming noticed a stranger pushing a cart laden with masks and costumes: a donkey suit, a chicken mask, and a metallic dress. It piqued his curiosity and he called out, "Hi there, what's in the cart?"

"I am a player in the theater. These are props for the picture show," the player replied.

"The picture show?" Charming inquired.

"It's a performance of players on a stage," the player explained. "While they do their thing, a panoramic picture scrolls behind them. It's exquisite! You should come tonight."

"With pleasure!" Charming cheered, and raced home to tell his family.

"I'm going to a picture show! Who wants to come with me?" he announced back in the throne room.

"I don't think so. Those can get wild," the king said.

"But—"

"I'll not have you risk our reputation." The king shut Charming down before he could even begin. "One day, you'll be the face of this great nation. We can't risk a blemish."

Charming huffed off.

"How would he know, he's such a bore," he pouted to himself. "He never plays games or takes risks, I doubt he has any quirks. . ." And in a moment of rebellion, Charming whistled for Laser and flew secretly to the picture show.

Charming found the theater and the show electrifying. The audience dressed with flair, and the performers with even more zest. The show included a peacock, a

66

swan that rose into the air on a rigging, and a sword fight! Charming was thrilled.

After the curtain call, the player who'd invited him motioned for Charming to join the actors backstage. There he found frenzied performers. They were in various states of dress, had comical makeup on, and were eating ravenously. It was nothing like the portrait sitting, waving in a parade, or modeling for the coin.

"I recognize you from the sweets campaign," noted the player who had been the peacock.

"Is it you on this coin?" a player dressed in a suit of armor asked as they tossed a gold piece.

"With all that modeling experience, you ever thought about trying your hand on the stage?" asked the player dressed as a swan.

Charming shook his head.

"I know a theater representative who'd love to meet you," the first player said. "Swing by tomorrow, I'll be waiting!"

So Charming made sure to appear.

"Allow me to introduce Buskin," the player announced upon Charming's arrival the next day. "You'll be in good hands with him."

"I run a professional stage company. With your life experience, I've a host of roles you'd be right for," Buskin explained.

"I'm game!" Charming exclaimed and with that, he jumped in with both feet. He practised sashaying across the floor, and he sang his heart out with his best rendition of "Twinkle Twinkle Little Star." Each day, he and Laser snuck away to attend auditions.

Charming auditioned to be a baker, a butcher, a candlestick maker, and a prince. He got the call back for the prince and won the role. Buskin was thrilled.

"I knew you had it in ya!" he proclaimed. "You'll be a star in no time!"

For the performance Charming only had one line. All he got to do was ride in on a white horse and slay a pathetic-looking papier-mache dragon. It wasn't what Charming had expected.

Charming then tried for roles as Little Pigs 1, 2, and 3 and a prince. He again got the role of the prince. Buskin again was tickled. But Charming was lukewarm. This role called for an old-fashioned costume. And one dull line: "I'm here to rescue you!" And he was supposed to lift up a bored princess in an impractical gown. None of which sat right with him. Anyways, at the audition the princess actress was better suited to lift him!

Charming was beginning to see a pattern. He tried out to be a dish, a spoon, and he even entered Laser to be a cow that jumped over a moon. Of course, because Buskin insisted and because he always got called back, he also auditioned for yet another prince role. He was cast, you guessed it, as the prince.

This time it was a bigger production. The costumer attached fake hair to his head, and gave him an ostentatious crown and massive fur. He could barely walk straight. He once again had only one line; "Have no fear, your prince is here!"

"This isn't acting," he thought. "I'm offended, to be honest," he complained to Buskin.

"I know you'd like to be considered for other roles," Buskin said. "But I thought you'd be glad to get so much work!"

"Is there nothing out there for me except one silly singular idea about what a prince is?" Charming spat.

"I don't want to see one version of my life repeated back to me. There are many different kinds of princes who can be played by different people. Why can't a prince play different people too?' he persisted.

Buskin listened carefully and pondered quietly.

"Maybe we should figure out what is special about you," he said. "What you bring to a role that no one else can. Do you have any hobbies?"

"Well, I used to, but my father asked that I spend less time on them. I used to be great at a fantasy card game. I was kind of an expert."

"Hey, I think know that card game! Golden Sword or something like that?"

"Knights of the Golden Shield! I loved all the twists and turns, and you could be so many different kinds of characters: monsters, princesses, kings and queens…"

"Here's a wild idea, what if we wrote an entirely new picture show, a live version of Knights of the Golden Shield?" Buskin thought aloud.

Charming perked up. "That sounds amazing!"

"I'll need to talk to some people," Buskin mused. "Let me see what I can do."

In the days that followed, Buskin and Charming outlined the show. The prince worked in the royal library and added details from his knowledge of the game. Buskin worked nearby in the garden. He observed the people of the court and castle and sought inspiration to make sure each role suited to any actor. Charming included his strong perspective on the roles of the royals.

"The prince must be shown not as a perfectly styled savior, but as a person with genuine interests and depth. A prince with their own distinction, with joy and affection to share and creativity that's celebrated!" Charming pronounced.

As the team worked, others looked on and soon the royal court was abuzz with murmurs of the project.

"I hear there is a new picture show in the works!" the lords and ladies nattered.

"I hear there will be loads of roles for all kinds of people," busied the staff.

Soon the chatter reached the king's ears. But he wasn't excited, he was irritated.

"A new picture show? I won't have it!" he complained. "Who's responsible for this?" He began to ask around. Soon, Buskin was summoned to the palace.

"Yes, your highness? Are you eager to produce the new show?" he asked.

"Produce, whatever are you thinking?" The king was alarmed.

"I've written it for your son, the prince. With him, really. He's added so many details. Would you like to read the casting call?" Buskin said, proudly handing over a long scroll.

The king looked confused but accepted the scroll. He unrolled it and read aloud:

"Open auditions! Exciting original staging of your favorite game, Knights of the Golden Shield, written by Prince Charming himself." The king raised his eyebrows. "Fancy taking the stage as Lord of the Manor in the comedic role of an era? Or stepping into the shoes of a queen who plays the drums, or making your own destiny as a princess who rescues a dragon in need?"

"Come as you are," a voice from the gallery spoke forth. "All ages and experiences eligible to play all roles."

The king and Buskin looked and saw that the voice belonged to Charming. He strode forth, his hair self-styled, a pen in his hand. "Dad, Buskin, I think I've found my new purpose as a leader. And it's not parading in front of the public anymore."

Both looked surprised.

"I'm not the one who needs to be seen," Charming explained. "Everyone knows who I am. It's time we started seeing all the people in our kingdom: in parades, on coins, in portraits, and in plays!"

"What brought all this on?" the king asked. "You have an amazing life as the face of the kingdom."

"Well, not quite," Charming said. "It's our people who are the true face of our land. And I've had to hide parts of myself. It's not right."

The king hung his head. He finally understood. For he, too, had suffered the same. "I used to make beautiful embroidery, but in all the portraits and manuscripts it was omitted because it wasn't seen as befitting a royal," he confessed. "You're right, we all need to be seen, fully with all our uniqueness. Now let's get this show up and running!"

Buskin and the king worked together to produce the show and Charming oversaw casting. He relished meeting people from the kingdom and pairing their special skills and interests with exciting roles.

Knights of the Golden Shield was an immediate hit. The kingdom loved the range of performances and the players loved the creative challenge. At the curtain call, Charming took the stage not as a player playing a part, but as a writer penning the truth: that anyone can don the crown, and everyone can play more than one role.

Knights of the Golden Shield was an immediate hit.

King Midas

Once upon a time, in a kingdom by a bright blue sea, there ruled a royal family named Midas. The king and queen enjoyed a fortune that included a generous garden, farm, and stables, and the best of education, entertainment, and art. They were respected for the way in which they shared these gifts to enrich the lives of their people.

While the queen traveled extensively to trade the royal resources, the king stayed at the palace to support the local people. When citizens fell on hard times or needed help, they came to the king with their worries. King Midas took great pride in making sure everyone had everything they needed. He saw to it that his kingdom was an upbeat place, where never a tear was shed, and he buried any less cheerful thought or grievance that came his way. After working with his royal advisors, Halide and Safiye, the king would spend time relaxing, reading, and playing in the garden with his son, Altin, with whom he was especially close.

Although contentment reigned within the kingdom and health and happiness were its maxim, life was not without unpleasantness. As time passed, it became harder and harder for King Midas to fix everything. An illness befell the land and though Midas built a hospital, he found it difficult to see his people feeling poorly. When a great storm flooded the beach, the king sent the stable staff to help relocate the seaside dwellers. He couldn't bear to see their pain first-hand. Unable to deal with the growing number of people who came to ask for his help, Midas shut his doors, telling his advisors to give out money on his behalf. But money couldn't fix all of the problems. It couldn't help people who had lost a loved one or who were simply feeling lonely and afraid. Midas sensed he was failing his people and he was rattled.

"How can I give so much, and yet people still feel sad or fall on hard times?" he wrote to his partner the queen one day.

After pacing around his quarters, he headed out to the garden to clear his head. Altin and some kids were on the green. At first it looked like they were playing, but upon closer inspection they were squabbling.

"Made ya look, made ya look, now you're in the dirty soot!" The children teased Altin, who had slipped near the fire pit.

"Enough!" the king bellowed. The children scattered, leaving Altin in tears.

It was the last straw. Midas couldn't bear to see Altin in pain.

"Everywhere I turn I find distress!" he lamented. "I wish my touch could keep everything in my kingdom as good as gold."

As soon as he had spoken, clouds crawled across the normally unblemished blue sky. Fearing a storm, Midas was about to duck inside when a blaze of lightning flashed. In it, something caught his eye. It was a face!

"I'm an Envoy of the Sky!" the grinning lightning bolt hailed.

"What?!" Midas shouted, alarmed.

"I heard your plea," the face replied.

"Plea?" Midas was confused.

"You'd like a touch that yields only goodness for the people of your kingdom," the Envoy said.

Midas nodded in awe.

"You long for a day when no one brings you their sadness," the Envoy confirmed.

"Yes, I want everyone to feel golden. To never have a cause for tears!" Midas described.

"Your wish is my command, but careful what you wish for," cautioned the Envoy.

With that, the Envoy vanished, and the sky cleared to reveal a hot midday sun. Bewildered, the king sought a place to sit. He reached out to a stone bench, and a peculiar thing happened. When Midas touched the stone, it turned instantly to gold, as if painted with a brush. Midas's eyes grew wide.

"Could it be?" he thought. "Has my wish to brighten the kingdom like gold come true?"

King Midas paced the gardens, looking to test his theory. An irritable peacock strode by, squawking. The king reached out and brushed its tailfeathers. The bird's tinny screech turned into a sweet song and the emerald and purple feathers transformed into gold.

Midas was speechless. He raced into the palace.

"OK," he thought. "My touch turns the appearance of things, but what about

73

feelings? That's what I really want to change."

The king sought his trusted advisors, Halide and Safiye. The two came at once, each with a long list of needs and concerns.

"King Midas, we are so glad you called," Safiye said.

"There are many people that need your attention," Halide followed up.

"Not to worry, I can fix this," the king said and laid a hand on the shoulder of each of them. As he did so, their clothing instantly became woven of golden thread and their hair and skin glittered with the kiss of the sun. Their very posture and disposition shifted too.

"What were you saying?" the king encouraged.

Safiye scrutinized her documents with wonderment. "Why, everything is . . . grand today."

"Only good news from me too," Halide confirmed, perplexed.

"Wonderful, take the rest of the day off, and tomorrow too!" beamed the king. "I'll see my visitors on my own."

The two advisors looked stumped, but accepted the king's wishes.

King Midas found a long line of citizens queued up to see him. Each had stress and urgency written on their faces.

"This morning, I shall greet each of you with a handshake!" the king proclaimed.

He trod down the line of visitors and shook each hand. As he did, each member of the community who had come seeking the king's help was graced instead with a new

golden glow, and clothes of fine gold thread. Most importantly, they no longer had anything unfavorable to say. There was no heartbreak, no difficult conversations, no painful decisions, or sad news.

The visitors quickly dispersed, and the king sat in silence at his desk. He reached for a pear as a snack. The skin of the fruit turned quickly to a matte gold. King Midas took a bite, expecting to find a sweet, juicy center. But he was repulsed to discover the flesh of the pear was sandy and tasteless.

"Huh," the king said to himself. "Maybe my taste buds are asleep." He spied a sweet fig with salty cheese inside. His favorite! "This will wake them up!" But once again as soon as King Midas touched the treat, the auburn fig turned a deep gold and the white soft cheese took on the appearance of gold leaf. When he bit into it, the sweet and savory morsel had a bland, pasty taste.

The king began to consider that there might be drawbacks to his magic touch. But his thoughts were interrupted by Altin who came to join him. Not thinking, the king drew his son near for a big bear hug and Altin too fell under the spell of Midas's magic touch. Altin's skin and hair glittered gold and his clothes turned a bright metallic. The king felt pleased when he considered that Altin might never again be burdened. But Altin hardly noticed, he seemed distracted.

"What are you up to today?" the king asked his son.

Altin just shrugged.

"Oh, come on, you must have something fun on the books. Friends coming to play?" the king asked cheerfully.

Altin looked glum.

"I usually have plans with other kids," he started. "But . . . recently they haven't been . . . ?" As Altin reached the end of the thought, his voice disappeared with a hiss like a candle being extinguished.

"What is it, my child? You can tell me anything!" King Midas said, alarm in his voice.

But when Altin opened his mouth, no sound came out.

King Midas realized with horror what had happened. "Oh no!" he cried out. "My son, you have a worry, something that has made you sad, and I, your loving parent, have taken away your ability to share it!"

With this realization, all the feelings King Midas had pushed away came rushing back. He felt sadness, just as his people had. He felt fear, just as his people had tried to share with him. A great swelling cry erupted within King Midas.

His face scrunched, his eyes watered, and his mouth opened. He moved his hands to wipe his cheeks and tears marked his palms.

Next, a curious thing happened. Midas felt the words his son wasn't able to speak form in his own mouth. For like his son, he too had once been teased.

"They haven't been treating you like a friend," the king said.

He reached out to hold his boy's hand. As he did, Altin's clothing returned to its original form and his hair and skin to their natural color.

"That's right, Father. How did you know?" Altin admitted, his voice breaking free.

"Because I too have been teased, and it hurts," the king reflected. The two sat quietly, together with their feelings.

"I was afraid to connect with the people of our kingdom. With their sadness and their worry," King Midas said. "I wanted to make it all go away and cover it with a pretty finish. But I know now that I can't stop life's peaks and valleys. I can't stop people feeling hurt. What I can do is be there, to feel with them and show them they don't have to be alone. Starting with you, my son."

The king and Altin shared a big hug. "If you share how you feel with your friends, I suspect they will want to do better. Now come, I've people to see!" The king swept Altin with him through the palace grounds and out to the streets of the city.

King Midas walked with purpose. He shook the hand of everyone he passed and sought out those on whom he'd bestowed the golden touch, restoring them to their usual selves. Then he pulled a few chairs about him in the town square.

"Sit with me, my people, your king is here to listen. I've felt the same feelings as you and I am right beside you," he said as he sat down.

The king's trusted advisors Safiye and Halide heard the commotion in the streets and came right away. They found King Midas most out of character. He looked as if he'd been crying. He held his son upon his lap and was sharing from his well of experience with a young man whose mother, a ship's captain, was far away at sea.

"I too get lonely," he said softly. "I miss my queen so much when she is away."

When he saw his advisors, he rose to place a hand on each of their shoulders, so that they too were returned to their natural form.

"Are you turning over a new leaf, dear King?" Safiye asked, wide-eyed.

"Yes! The leaf of empathy!" the king announced. "Even though it can be difficult to hear people's pain, I'll never wish it away, not for all the gold in the world."

"We are here for you, King," Halide assured him.

"Actually," King Midas suggested, "let's be here for each other."

"Sit with me my people, your king is here to listen."

The Pied Piper

Centuries ago, when the land was dotted with tiny villages, there stood the town of Hemelin. In the town lived a family called Pappenheim. Perry Pappenheim traveled often as an ambassador of the minister's office. Pip Pappenheim was an at home parent and maintained a rad collection of instruments, specifically flutes and pipes.

The couple had ten lively children called Cuthbert, Corinne, Cory, Carlos, Corcoran, Carmen, Catriona, Casey, Culligan, and Caspar. Each had a sweet cat of their very own to form a special bond with. As a bonus, they kept vermin away. The cats were called Kit, Kerry, Klutch, Kwik, Khrys, Kepnes, Kipper, Koffee, Kaia, and King.

At the start of each day, Pip fed the kitties, coached the children to do chores, and styled their hair. While the children were at school, he selected books from the library and sewed toys for the cats. When the children returned from school, Pip sat among them as they did their homework. He peeled children off the floor when they roiled in frustration and plucked cats from the furniture.

Pip taught the kids to swim, cycle, dance, wrestle, tie their shoes, and cook an egg. He was there for every dinner and dessert. Every laugh and tickle, scrape and scream, doctor's visit and fever dream. Pip never missed a performance, competition, or recital. The kids could always spot their father cheering them on since he wore a rockin' pied jacket.

Once the children were tucked in bed, and the cries of, "Father, I need help," faded to the sleepy words of, "I love you Father, good night," Pip's bonus work began. He did the dishes and the laundry. He heated an iron and pressed the linens. He prepped special lunches to suit quirky diets. He settled bills and took care of repairs. And when the kitties brought the gift of a mouse, Pip would take care of that too.

When the day neared its end, Pip and Perry relaxed together: reading, making music, and making each other laugh. Pip played his pipes and made up funny songs about the imperfections of the day: *"Today the weather was so grim, I had to take the kitties in, they spilled their food across the floor, so each kid slipped coming in the dooooooor."*

The cats liked to circle Pip's feet and sway to the tune. They'd follow him in a little train as he traipsed around the house, perfecting his composition. It became the talk of the town as people loved sharing cute cat anecdotes. The talk even made its way to the minister's chambers.

One night, as Perry put the kids to bed before a business trip, there was a knock on the door. It was the minister.

"You must be looking for Perry," Pip said. "Shall I get her?"

The cats liked to circle Pip's feet and sway to the tune.

"It's not her I need, it's you," the minister stated.

"Me?" Pip was surprised.

"Our town requires your help! A menace of rodents has befallen Hamelin. They are festering in the schoolhouse and nibbling in the cheesemongers. Contaminating the well and nesting in the eaves. Good swift exterminators are needed urgently," the minister explained. "Cats that can catch vermin."

Pip didn't understand at first.

"Play your pipe," the minister prompted.

So, Pip put the pipe to his lips and began to play a tune. As he played the cats climbed down from railings and ledges. They came out of nooks and from under couches. They swooped and danced at Pip's feet.

"I think I know what you have in mind," Pip said, putting down his pipe. "You want me to use our cats as exterminators?"

"You and your cats are the only ones for the job. Plus, you're just at home all day, right?" the minister said.

"Who will take over for me at work?" Pip asked. "With Perry away too?"

"Work? Ah, we'll send someone to help with the kids. It can't be all that difficult. We'll even throw in a little payment in return for you stepping away from your 'work,'" the minister offered.

"Well, alright then," Pip replied reluctantly. "I'm glad to help our town."

Early the next day, Pip put on his jacket, gathered his pipe, and went into the streets of Hamelin. He put the pipe to his lips, and a train of cats followed him.

Kit snagged a rodent near the clock tower. Kerry corraled one near the well. Klutch, Kwik, and Khrys rounded up a few near the cheese shop. While Kepnes ran one off the pier, Kipper and Koffee cornered vermin by the schoolhouse and Kaia pounced on one in the market. Silly King just batted one in the town square like a toy.

Pip played on and the cats fell into a tidy procession. They propeled the rodents ahead of them and traveled over a day until they reached a muddy mountain. There Pip ceased the piping. He and the cats left the rodents to relocate and began the long journey home.

Pip and the kitties returned to a warm reception from the citizens of Hamelin. The minister offered a hearty hug and whispered,

"Grateful for your service. I hope you'll accept this gesture as payment." The minister gestured to the crowd.

Pip was confused. "Gesture? I thought you were going to pay me for the time I was away?"

He shelved his quarrel however when he saw the street lined with smiling children eager to shake his hand. At the end of the receiving line Pip found his own children. He was delighted to see them after a few days away but noticed right away that something was amiss.

Cuthbert had no socks. Corinne had matted braids. Cory was covered in jam stains and Carlos held soaking wet school books. Corcoran and Carmen were wearing the wrong glasses. Catriona was eating her breakfast in the afternoon. Casey and Casper had singed eyebrows and Culligan had sewn his needle-point craft to his pants, hoop and all!

"What happened while I was gone?" Pip wondered to himself.

It was even worse inside the Pappenheim home. Pip came home to a sink piled high with dishes. Every child had a project that needed immediate attention, and not one had brushed their teeth or eaten a vegetable.

"I can't be gone for two days without this place falling into ruin?" Pip's temperature rose. "I must have a word with the minster!" And off he stormed.

"Oh rats!" Perry exclaimed when she too arrived home and surveyed the mess. She asked a neighbor to watch the children, and went after Pip, to be by his side.

The Pappenheims barged into the minister's chambers and demanded to be heard.

"I thought we were meant to have some help," Perry said. "Pip did this great favor for the town and it doesn't look at all like anyone was helping our family."

The minister looked taken aback.

"Pip, Sir, I am very grateful for your efforts ridding us of rodents," defended the minister. "I didn't think your flock required much. I mean, how hard can it be? Surely they can't fill all your time?"

"I work morning to night so that our family can succeed!" Pip steamed. "I've done a great service for this community. Not only in driving out the rodents, but also in supporting all the endeavors of my children. They are the future of this place!"

"Oh . . ." began the Minister.

"It's not OK to trivialize Pip's job," Perry said. "Running our home is just as key a profession as anyone else's and Pip deserves recognition for it."

"I wonder what the town would make of a walkout. If all the parents that kept homes were to leave like the rats from the streets," Pip said sternly.

"Well now, let's not be hasty," the minister tried.

But Pip was hasty. In fact, he was out of the door and down the road. He drew a small pipe from his pocket and blew furiously. Doors opened around Hamelin, and busy hard-working parents of all kinds joined in the streets. At-home parents, grandparents, business people, soldiers, farmers, teachers. They stood together in solidarity.

"People of Hamelin!" Pip announced. "There are unseen anchors in this town. Parents who work in our homes, without whom our town would float away. If you too wish to recognize their contribution, join me in a strike!"

"We stand beside you!" said a lawyer, putting down his papers and robe. "I'll gladly support my husband so he can strike with you!"

"Count me in," the postal carrier's partner spoke. "Forget the mail, I'm the one en-route now." And they too put down their work.

More and more stay-at-home parents joined the cause. They threw down their aprons, clipboards, and kitchen gloves. Perry distributed instruments from Pip's collection and the hard-working men and women strode off together in harmony, music trailing behind them.

"Let's see how you last a day without us!" Pip called back.

"Come back!" shouted the minister, chasing Pip down the street. But it was too late.

The next day fell off course quickly. Children arrived at school per usual, but the adults ran late, disorganized and tired. They could scarcely keep the town afloat. Mail went undelivered, shops went un-stocked, the milk was delivered so late it went bad, and everyone was cross.

The minister was especially affected. Few of the staff were on hand since many were filling gaps at home. Perry was only able to make one meeting before she had to take a child to swimming then help with a rehearsal and ref a game. Not to mention the fact that she always had something in her hands, from sewing buttons to decorating cookies to cleaning up spills in the kitchen.

The minister was really concerned. They couldn't have a successful town under these circumstances. The strike with the families needed resolving. With a fresh perspective, the minister rose early the next day. Foregoing town business, he instead visited each house in Hamelin with a warm message.

"We are all equally worthy of recognition. What I thought was ordinary is in fact extraordinary." The final visit was at the Pappenheims, where Pip had returned in the wee hours to be reunited with his loved ones.

"Your absence allowed my heart to grow and my perspective to broaden," the minister explained. "I'd like to offer you a paid role in on-call pest control. With a parent support team to step in whenever you are away providing this important service." The minister stretched out his hand.

"Parent support team?" Pip queried.

"I see how amazing the network of parents is in Hamelin," the minister said, nodding in Perry's direction. "I want to make it official, so every townsperson can participate in raising our children, serve the community and lead a balanced life."

Pip agreed to the new terms with a strong handshake.

So it was that the town of Hamelin came to have an official town-wide parent cooperative. Because of Pip and his peers, no family went without support when they needed it. The town flourished with a long tradition of music too. With the help of some friends, Pip formed a stellar band and wrote a lot of cute cat tunes. To showcase Hamelin's built-in pest control, the Pappenheim kids painted a new town sign that read: *Welcome to Hamelin, Proud Home of the Pied Piper.* It featured the town mascot "King the Kitty."

The Elves and the Shoemaker

Once upon a time, in a tiny shop in a fusty corner of a brooding metropolis, a great mystery occurred.

The city was bustling and demanding. Its streets burst with people from all over the world. The tiny shop of note was sandwiched in an alley known as Cobbler's Row—a street lined with stores that offered footwear. One had shoes for fitness, another for business, another for sport. There was a sandal shop and one for special occasions and costumes. One carried slippers, another only boots.

But the shop that lay host to the mystery made one-of-a-kind slip-on shoes. They were leather and extensively embroidered with gold and silver thread. The design had been a trade secret for hundreds of years. The shop always shared its prosperity, donating shoes to the Children's Society, and to people who called the streets their home.

The shoemaker in the tiny shop was called Lyman. He had a smooth line for a mouth and wore a hat low over his brow. He whistled melancholy airs to himself while he worked, because sadly, in recent years, visitors to Lyman's shop never stayed long enough to buy anything. What had once been a thriving brand was facing extinction, and Lyman was quite poor.

"I wish I could have upheld the tradition of generosity this shop had as its legacy," Lyman mourned, "but now I am the one who is in need."

One dark and rainy night, as Lyman prepared to close the shop for good, something caught his eye. It was a small box. Inside he found a portion of leather, trimmings, and beads. Some of the very best materials, mementos from when he started out.

It was just enough to make one last pair of shoes. Lyman dutifully measured and cut the materials. He recalled his younger self as a new cobbler as he worked. But he was too tired to continue. So he went to bed in his loft above the shop, resolving to finish the shoes in the morning.

When the sun rose, Lyman returned to the final project. But upon seeing his workbench, he froze. For there, gleaming in the sunlight were the shoes—completely finished!

Lyman picked up the shoes to examine them more closely. They were so well made. Every stitch was fashioned expertly. It was as if someone had slipped into his mind, Lyman thought. Then it occurred to Lyman, perhaps someone had actually slipped into the shop!

Lyman panicked. He backed away from the shoes suspiciously.

"Help! I've been . . . burgled!" he cried.

People came running at once. Someone blew a whistle and the constabulary arrived, two detectives, Clog and Mule. They whipped out magnifying glasses and notebooks and took in the scene.

"Why do you think you've been burgled?" they asked Lyman.

"It's these shoes," Lyman explained. "Last night they were in pieces and now look!"

"Ummm . . . That sounds like the opposite of a robbery," mused Detective Clog.

"There are no signs of a break in. . . ." Detective Mule surmised.

"Someone was here," Lyman protested.

"If there's no evidence of a crime, our work here is done," Detective Clog concluded blandly, and the detectives departed.

Lyman refused to accept this. He got down on the floor and looked for clues. He spotted a disturbance in the dust. Upon examination, it appeared to be a tiny footprint.

Lyman was wondering who it might belong to when he was interrupted by a customer.

"Excuse me? These shoes are divine! I see they are the last pair. I'll give you 100 for them," a stylish gentleman said.

Lyman was shocked. That was big money. It was enough for him to make another pair, even a second he could donate. So he accepted the generous offer.

That evening, Lyman cut out two remarkable shoes, unlike anything he'd done before. Oddly, the challenge brought a smile to his face. It was something he hadn't felt in years. As before, intending to continue his work the next morning, Lyman left the project in pieces and went to bed.

When he awoke, Lyman was met with a familiar yet still arresting sight. Again, where he had left only cut materials, sat two completed pairs of shoes!

He knew the constabulary would be of no help, so instead he called his former mentor Ötzi. Ötzi had years of experience and while he was nearly blind from the detailed labor, and his joints were tight and tender, he was always there for a former apprentice.

"I need your help with a mystery!" Lyman explained. "I left out unfinished work and woke to find it flawlessly completed. Look!" He held up the two pairs of shoes.

Ötzi's curiosity was piqued. "Have you looked around for clues?"

"I found a little print on the floor, a tiny smudge. I'll show you." Lyman grabbed his magnifying glasses and Ötzi put the loupe to his eye.

Sure enough, the smudge remained right where Lyman had seen it. Only this time it was not alone. Alongside it sat an identical little smudge.

Ötzi stared. "It looks like a set of footprints."

"But whose?" Lyman worried.

Their discussion was interrupted by two customers who had spotted the shoes.

"Those are divine!" said one friend to another.

"Both traditional and cutting edge!" the friend replied. "You know who would flip over them?"

"Why, the City Kids' sports programme," said the first.

"Indeed! We'd like to purchase these shoes for 400 and commission a set of five for an organization we are patrons of. Would 1000 cover that?" said the second.

Lyman was speechless, so Ötzi accepted on his behalf.

"How am I going to make four pairs of shoes by tomorrow?!" Lyman said, aghast.

"Oh, don't worry. I'll lend a hand," offered Ötzi.

The two set to work. Lyman found materials, including cool bits of flare he knew the kids would appreciate, while Ötzi sharpened tools. Together they cut and measured patterns.

"It's been so long since I've been busy and had company in the shop," Lyman mused. "This is really nice. I almost wish I didn't have to close the place."

"What makes you think you need to close? Seems to me you've plenty of business," Ötzi observed.

"Huh," thought Lyman.

Ötzi was getting on in years and his eyes tired quickly so they quit early. Lyman bid his mentor good night and retired. Content to finish the shoes in the morning, he soon fell fast asleep. He was awoken early the next day by a banging on the shop window. It was Ötzi. Lyman raced to let him in.

"What is it?" Lyman asked urgently. But Ötzi merely pointed.

Lyman followed Ötzi's finger to a row of pristine and polished new shoes fit for active kids. Exquisitely sewn and expertly finished with lightning rod details. Beside the shoes he could see not one, not two, but four tiny smudges. More footprints!

Lyman and Ötzi exchanged awed looks. But they scarcely had time to investigate, for word had quickly spread that Lyman was newly inspired and back in business. A line had formed outside the shop. The line outside turned the flat line of Lyman's mouth into a long overdue smile. All the midnight magic was beginning to change him. His work was enthusiastic, and it spoke to people.

Lyman hired Ötzi and they came to specialize in overnight orders. Whatever they cut out in the evening was always finished the following morning. Both soon became quite wealthy.

They were able to return the brand to its status as a donor of shoes to those in need. One day they received a warm thank-you card from a recipient. But the acknowledgment left them feeling empty, as the success wasn't theirs alone.

"It doesn't feel right," Lyman said. "I don't know who to thank for our success."

"We need to solve this mystery before someone else does," Ötzi said. "Let's stay up tonight to see who is giving us this helping hand."

Lyman agreed and that night the two—veiled in dark trench coats—lay in wait. Just as Ötzi was about to nod off, Lyman nudged him. There, creeping from the shadows into the moonlight, strode four shifty . . . Elves?! They were barefoot and wore only paper bags as clothes, which rustled as they stepped. Why, they weren't scary at all. In fact, they were rather gentle and jovial.

The elves took their place at the workbench, picked up the cut-out pieces and worked so unbelievably quickly and nimbly Ötzi and Lyman couldn't look away. The elves did not stop until they had finished everything. Then they placed the completed shoes on the workbench, and quickly ran away.

"It's elves who have breathed new life into the shop, into me in fact!" Lyman whispered.

"It's elves we've to thank," wondered Ötzi.

"We must show them our appreciation," Lyman said.

"But how?' Ötzi asked.

"I've got it!" Lyman jumped into action. He gathered scraps from the work room. "They were nearly bare, all they had were those paper bags. Let's sew some clothes for them."

"I can knit stockings, and we should make shoes for each of them too," Ötzi added.

The following evening, when everything was finished, Lyman and Ötzi set their presents out instead of unfinished work. Then they hid in their trench coats again. At midnight the elves came skipping in, ready to start their work. When they saw the little clothes instead, they at first seemed puzzled, but then delighted. They quickly put them on, and sang:

We're dressed in our attire you see,

No longer little cobblers we be!

Their song complete, the elves scampered out of the shop, and never did return.

With the mystery dispelled and the elves unbound, Lyman and Ötzi reflected on what they would do next.

"We can't keep up with overnight orders, but you can still make great footwear," Ötzi said.

"Actually, what inspired me most was being able to help; to provide shoes for those in need. Even making those clothes for the elves. It brought my heart back to life," Lyman said.

"What're you saying?" Ötzi asked.

"I'd like to convert the shop into a space devoted to spreading goodwill and connecting the community with clothes and shoes. We all have ways we can help one another, and this is mine. No matter how small we may be or feel."

The two soon launched The Shoemakers' Secret, a house of philanthropy and service dedicated to making sure everyone in the city, from the youngest to the eldest, had access to shoes and clothing if they needed it. No matter the season and no matter the reason and no matter the size.

*When they saw the little clothes instead, they at
first looked puzzled, then delighted.*

Anansi

In ancient times, there lived a character whose story has been told for hundreds of years. Whose roguish qualities and playful nature shaped his time and his people. His name was Anansi.

Anansi had a big personality and liked to hear himself talk. He spun wonderful stories that captured the attention of everyone he met. He gestured with drama and accentuated with his wiry arms and long fingers; he was like a spider spinning a web.

People lingered on his every word. They listened patiently when his advice was spot on. His recommendation for curing a cold was well conceived. He made an excellent substitute teacher, as he kept all the kids laughing. And, with his collection of colorful town anecdotes, he was a great tour guide. Anansi even charmed the animals: dogs curled at his feet and warthogs rolled over to have their bellies scratched. Since he had everyone's ear and fancied himself knowledgeable on just about everything, he also had an opinion on nearly everything too.

When it was time for a town project, he broadcast:

"This place needs a stadium, let me tell you."

He had a judgment on every wedding match;

"Yeah, they're much too young," or, "I tell you who they should marry."

Even old scholars weren't immune to his unsolicited advice.

"You're lecturing chemistry, I'm well read on the subject. You know some say I discovered . . ." He could easily overtake conversation.

"I hear Anansi reads ten books a day in just as many languages," speculated a man cooling off with an icy drink.

"No way, he has a melon filled with the wisdom of the ancestors hidden in a tree only he can climb! That's why he knows so much," countered the man's dining companion.

"I think he's overrated. If he really knows everything, why he is hanging out with us?" joked a playful youth at the bar.

This youth was not alone in their thinking. Probably because they were one of Anansi's six children. And children are the first to point out when their parents aren't cool. Anansi's children were Goliath, Red, Golden Silk, Cam, Wolf, and Taran. Each was talented and hardworking in their own interests.

Goliath was an athlete and stone thrower, Golden Silk a weaver who adorned themselves in trains and capes. Cam was intuitive and sensitive, always feeling things deeply and able to spot trouble from miles away. Red was an expert hunter, butcher, and chef. Wolf was a shrewd builder and engineer, and always looking for ways

to make things better and stronger. Little Taran was drawn to water and recorded patterns in rivers and streams.

The children loved their father, but rolled their eyes at his know-it-all nature. Anansi brimmed with knowledge yet didn't know how to slow down and appreciate the expertise of his children.

"Leave that water nonsense," he'd say to Taran. "That'll never get you anywhere. Work on your people skills."

"Goliath, you're plenty big, why don't you push yourself as a wrestler?" he'd say as he posed. "I could have been a professional, I could teach you a thing or two."

"Cam, you look like a wildebeest, if you focused less on others, you'd have more time for your grooming routine," he'd preen, touching his own hair.

One day, Anansi went on a journey. His children were grateful for a respite from his know-it-all nonsense. His destination was a long way from home. Of course, Anansi didn't take advice on how to get there, and naturally got lost immediately.

As the hours wore on and darkness fell, so did Anansi! Right into a deep crevasse. In the crevasse, waiting in the darkness, lay a crocodile. Its jaw unhinged to welcome Anansi. There he sat facing his certain demise, all alone with not a soul to witness his dilemma.

Well, almost alone. For although he was far away, Cam sensed that Anansi was in trouble.

"Father is in danger!" Cam called to the others.

"Are you serious?" Taran complained.

"I'll bet he went unprepared," sighed Red.

"How bad is it, does he need help?" Wolf asked.

Cam nodded.

So the six children of Anansi undertook the rescue of their father. Cam divined just how far Anansi had gone and determined where he might be.

"Follow me!" Wolf paved a road with wooden boards and stone slabs.

The way was clumsy with many twists and turns. The six siblings plodded through the night, into dense forest and across a river. Finally, they came upon a jagged array of rocks and boulders, like teeth poking up from the mouth of the earth.

"This is it!" Cam announced. They began to call for their father.

After a while, when no response was heard, the group grew fearful.

"Where is he?" said Red.

"Quiet," said Goliath. "I hear breathing."

The group walked to a gaping crack and peered below. There, they discovered a great crocodile. Their father protruded from its open mouth!

"Father, are you OK?" Cam exclaimed.

A muffled affirmative could be heard.

"I think they are both stuck," Taran spoke up.

"If I could reach in there, I could gently take care of that croc. But I can't without falling in myself," explained Red.

"I think I can figure out a way to divert the river we passed. We can flush them both out," Taran suggested.

With Taran's direction, the six moved boulders and rocks to divert the path of the river. It was a long haul and even though the night was dark and cold, much sweat was spilt. After several hours, the faint trickle of water could be heard in the once dry area.

The group raced to the crevasse where their father waited in the crocodile. They watched as the river arrived and flooded the crevasse. Soon the crocodile wriggled free and floated up to a level where Red could reach it.

With a swift tug Red wrangled the beast and sat astride it like a horse. The others watched with unease. Red carefully coaxed the crocodile's jaw open and the rest of the crew pulled Anansi out to safety.

The group were relieved to have their father returned to them. They embraced and patted one another on the back.

"That was incredible!" said Cam.

"Couldn't have done it without you," said Wolf.

"You're a regular croc whisperer," said Goliath to Red.

"Taran's the genius," said Red.

"That was intense," said Taran.

"Glad that's over," said Golden Silk with a sigh.

Anansi, on the other hand, played it off like it was no big deal.

"Not your average walk in the woods, eh?" he boasted.

The rest stared in disappointment.

"Are you not even going to give us a thank you?" Goliath started.

"For what? I was just about to get myself out of that predicament. I was negotiating with the crocodile. You know me, I speak the language of animals."

The rest of the family let out a collective groan.

Suddenly, a great gust swept over the family. Everyone ducked except for Anansi. Which was most unlucky, because it wasn't a breeze, it was the draft of a great bird! It was larger than any vulture or eagle and it reached right out and grasped Anansi in its claws.

Anansi wriggled and thrashed, he kicked and pawed at the talons that held him, but to no avail. The bird was strong and it climbed into the air.

"Quick, what can we do?!" shouted Wolf.

"Help me gather stones!" called Goliath.

The team bent along the ground and filled their fists with rocks. Goliath flipped their shirt into a pouch, and all helped fill it with knuckle-sized stones. Then with eyes to the sky, Goliath in a flurry of force pelted the stones in the direction of the bird. The great beast dodged, it swerved, and it dove. Anansi remained in its grip. The bird climbed higher into a shield of clouds.

There was one final stone in the arsenal. Eyes closed, and with a deep breath, Goliath shot the stone like an arrow into the clouds above. The stone made contact, and moments later they heard the cry of a man.

"Aaaaaaaaaaaaaaaaah!"

The sound grew louder and closer and Anansi appeared above them in the sky. He was falling fast.

"Heeeeeeeelp meeeeeeeee," Anansi's voice cried out.

"Now he wants our help?" an exasperated Wolf let slip.

Swiftly and quietly Golden Silk ran forward, tearing the fabric train from their waist. It was their own design, beautiful flowers and stripes. The fabric billowed in the breeze as Golden Silk ran. The rest of the siblings understood at once what needed to be done.

They raced to the perimeter of the fabric and grabbed hold. Above them Anansi hurtled toward the earth. The six stretched the fabric taut to form a parachute. As soon as they had done so, their father struck the cloth. Anansi bounced in the air and then landed safely onto the luxurious fabric.

Anansi lay in the parachute overwhelmed with gratitude. He cried happy tears, and everyone climbed in beside him. The family held each other. Anansi kissed each and every one of his children.

"How ever did you know how to help me?" Anansi wept as he looked to the sky. "I thought I'd never see your faces again. That I'd miss the wonderful things you do."

The seven of them lay side by side. A full moon rose above and shone its soothing light upon them.

"What can I give you to repay each of you for the ways in which you have rescued me today?' Anansi pondered aloud. "If I could, I would pull the moon from the sky for you all."

"We don't need anything, Father," Golden Silk said.

"Speak for yourself," joked Wolf.

"Seriously, I must give you something!" Anansi insisted.

"Why don't you let us give to *you* for a change?" Red said gently.

Anansi went very quiet.

"You can give us the chance to teach you, Father," Cam added.

Anansi saw the new path he needed to take. "I'll leave the moon in the sky," he joked, "and I'll let my children shine on me for a change."

In the days and years that followed Anansi was true to his promise. He offered his children the reward of his time as a gracious listener. A "know it not" rather than a "know it all." Anansi saw that people appreciated listening far more than instructions.

And as for Golden Silk's torn train, well the family spun a new tapestry. It featured each of them, Anansi too, as gardeners tending an orchard in the mind of a great thinker.

"You can give us the chance to teach you, Father,"
Cam added.

In the spirit of Washington Irving's words, "There is a sacredness in tears. They are not the mark of weakness but of power. They are messengers of overwhelming grief and of unspeakable love."–V. M.

To my husband, my best supporter and the kindest, bravest man I know–J. B.

Brimming with creative inspiration, how-to projects, and useful information to enrich your everyday life, Quarto Knows is a favourite destination for those pursuing their interests and passions. Visit our site and dig deeper with our books into your area of interest: Quarto Creates, Quarto Cooks, Quarto Homes, Quarto Lives, Quarto Drives, Quarto Explores, Quarto Gifts, or Quarto Kids.

High-five to the Hero © 2019 Quarto Publishing plc. Text © 2019 Vita Murrow. Illustrations © 2019 Julia Bereciartu.

First published in 2019 by Frances Lincoln Children's Books, an imprint of The Quarto Group, 400 First Avenue North, Suite 400, Minneapolis, MN 55401, USA. T (612) 344-8100 F (612) 344-8692 **www.QuartoKnows.com**

The right of Vita Murrow to be identified as the author and Julia Bereciartu to be identified as the illustrator of this work has been asserted by them in accordance with the Copyright, Designs and Patents Act, 1988 (United Kingdom).

A catalogue record for this book is available from the British Library.

ISBN 978-1-78603-782-4

The illustrations were created in watercolor, gouache, and colored pencil
Set in Bembo Roman Infant

Published by Rachel Williams
Designed by Karissa Santos
Edited by Katie Cotton
Production by Nicolas Zeifman

Manufactured in Guangdong, China TT062018

1 3 5 7 9 8 6 4 2